DENZEL'S LIPS

Also by Anita Diggs

A Meeting in the Ladies' Room

A Mighty Love

The Other Side of the Game

DENZEL'S LIPS

ANITA DIGGS

Dafina
BOOKS

KENSINGTON PUBLISHING CORP.

http://www.kensingtonbooks.com

DAFINA BOOKS are published by

Kensington Publishing Corp.
850 Third Avenue
New York, NY 10022

ISBN 0-7582-1051-5

First Kensington Trade Paperback Printing: October 2006
10 9 8 7 6 5 4 3 2 1

Printed in the United States of America

For Michele,
wherever you are

Author's Note

Asha and Saundra were first introduced to the literary world in *The Other Side of the Game.* I did not intend to write about Saundra again. *Denzel's Lips* was supposed to be Asha's story, but I received many, many e-mails asking about Saundra, Yero, and Phillip. Readers wanted to know if Saundra ever heard from Evelyn again. They also wondered if Phillip ever got back in his daughter's good graces.

I realized that Asha and Saundra, like most sisters, are connected forever. So here is the second part of their story. Enjoy!

PART ONE

THE LADIES

Chapter 1

ASHA

Why did my new mother-in-law have to be such a bitch? I wondered as I washed the breakfast dishes. Yesterday we had New Year's Eve dinner at her house, which is up in Scarsdale, New York, twenty-seven miles away. She started her shit as soon as Nick and I walked through the door. First, she wanted to know why I hadn't returned a phone call from one of her cronies. I told her for the umpteenth time that I am not a committee person. I mean, come on, imagine me all trussed up in some boring-ass business suit, drinking coffee and eating pastries while trying to figure out how to save the world. She pursed up her mean little lips and asked why I don't care about the throwaway teenaged girls who live at the Monday's Child Group Home. It isn't that I don't care. It simply isn't in my nature to try and get people to do what they don't want to do. And I was sure that those unfortunate girls did not want a bunch of wealthy females telling them how to get their lives in order. Then she wanted to know why I was wearing two earrings in each ear. I explained that it was part of my new look. I wanted to add that it was none of her goddamn business, but Nick's eyes warned me not to break on his mother. The capper was when we were enjoying after-dinner martinis. She complained that Nick and I had married in haste. That we should have waited until the Seabrook clan got to know me better. What she really meant was that there hadn't been enough time for her to talk Nick out of tying the knot with me.

I'd had enough.

I slammed my martini glass down on her antique coffee table and stood up. It was time for me to go. Nick tried to make peace. I told him in no uncertain terms that he could either drive us home or I was taking the car and he could walk his punk ass back. Either way, I was out of there.

We left.

Nick didn't say a word all the way home and he still had an attitude.

All my life I've avoided getting involved with the mama of whoever I was dating. Guys would ask me to meet their mama and I'd say no. There was only one time that I made an exception. A guy named Randy got me to his family's Thanksgiving feast and his mama was nice. But that was the only time I took the chance.

Randy ended up killing himself a month later when I dumped him. Sometimes, I think I should go see his mother and tell her how sorry I am, but he died a whole year ago. What would be the point after all this time?

My own mother had a stroke and died when I was very young. We didn't have a chance to go through the mother/daughter fights over who was good enough to date me.

Nick and I met through one of my old coworkers. Sort of. I used to be an accessories buyer at Macy's Department Store. I'm not big on female friendships, but I talked to this girl named Amy a lot because she was just out of college and was far away from her family, who lived in Los Angeles. She also had no self-esteem whatsoever. Well, one day she came into my office, looking all pumped up. She was so excited, she was practically bouncing off the walls. The first thing I noticed was the huge grin on her face. Then the sparkle in her eyes. Then the fact that her hair was freshly done. Finally, I realized that Amy was wearing a pink sleeveless dress and a beautiful pair of flat, matching sandals. Her yellow skin should have looked washed out, but it didn't. She looked beautiful and I told her so. Curious, I asked what was going on.

Amy said that she'd met a guy online. His name was Nick Seabrook and he was smart, black, handsome, and rich. They had been e-mailing each other like crazy for months and now they had a date. He was taking her to dinner at the Four Seasons, which is one of the most expensive restaurants in New York City.

Nick sounded like my type of guy.

Then Amy said that his family owned a chain of restaurants. When she said they were called Seabrook Soul Food, the name clicked right away. There was one on Lenox Avenue in Harlem. I had eaten there a million times.

Now I knew for sure that Nick was my type of guy.

When she started wringing her hands because Nick didn't know what she looked like, an idea started forming in my busy brain. It seemed that Nick had sent her an electronic picture, but she had been too insecure to send one back.

They were supposed to meet in front of the restaurant at six thirty.

An hour later, I dumped a huge amount of work on Amy. I told her it was a departmental emergency that couldn't wait. I promised that she could leave by seven o'clock.

Then I jumped in a cab.

Nick Seabrook turned out to be gorgeous.

I told him that my name was really Asha Mitchell and that I used the whole Amy thing as a precaution. I said that my whole family history was made up and that I was really a native New Yorker. A woman has to be careful with all the nuts victimizing women during the whole Internet dating thing, I explained.

He understood.

Needless to say, I couldn't let him take me into the Four Seasons because Amy was going to show up sooner or later. So I convinced him to try a swank Italian place about twenty blocks away. He turned out to be funny, sweet, and very, very interested in me. I took him back to my place after dinner and screwed his brains out.

Once he was gone, I paced the floor wondering what to do about Amy. She would probably e-mail him, asking why he stood her up. How could I stop her?

I couldn't.

So I marched into work the following morning and told her the truth. She burst into tears, cursed me out, and quit her job on the spot.

Saundra, my sister, told me that my behavior had been scandalous.

Whatever.

Nick and I got together every time he was in town. He was generous, we partied hearty, and the sex was great. When I finally told him the truth, he thought it was funny.

So I didn't lose a wink of sleep over Saundra's disapproval.

Three months later, the man was hooked. I mean, seriously in love. That didn't work for me. He was cool but not cool enough for me to give up my other lovers. After I set him straight, he went back to his player ways. I dated other men. He dated other women. Everything was fine. The strain didn't get to him until nine months later and then he put his foot down. Either I was going to become his woman or it was time to say good-bye.

If he wasn't sole heir to the Seabrook Soul Food fortune, I would have shown his ass the door. But I'm nobody's fool.

That all happened a year ago.

We're married now and when his bitchy mother and henpecked father go on to glory, Nick will inherit a heap of money, fourteen thriving soul food restaurants, a fleet of cars, and their mansion in Scarsdale.

For now, I am able to concentrate on decorating my five bedroom house while Nick goes off to work each morning. Our new house was a wedding present from his parents. For a girl like me who grew up dirt-poor in a run-down tenement building, it is a dream come true.

Chapter 2

SAUNDRA

Yero Brown is my husband of two years and I'm worried that he might be clinically depressed. He is a tall, thin man who, until recently, went straight to the gym after work, played basketball with his brother once a week, and always wanted to make love. About six months ago, he stopped going to the gym. He said it made him feel tired for hours afterward. Then one day his brother, Khari, came by to pick him up for a game and Yero just stretched and burrowed even farther beneath the covers. As far as sex is concerned, forget it. He doesn't seem to have much desire, and when it does happen, he feels wiped out for a day and a half.

I would talk to my sister, Asha, about this but she has recently moved out of New York City to Hercsville, Long Island, a suburb about an hour away. It is a community filled with wealthy black people and big houses. After years of working and looking out for herself, Asha finally has the life she always wanted, and I don't want to rain on her parade.

When Mama had a stroke and died, Asha was just past her eighteenth birthday, so she kept the apartment and worked two fast food jobs to pay the rent while she went to college at night.

Things were easier for me.

The Department of Social Services decided that Asha couldn't keep me since I was only sixteen. I moved in with my father, who was a police detective and owned his own house.

We have the same mama but two different daddies.

Asha's own father was dead and his family didn't even ask her if they could help out. Life was hard for Asha until she got her associate's degree.

Daddy paid my tuition and told me I didn't have to work until I got my bachelor's degree in fashion design. So Yero got a job at the post office and saved money for us to set up housekeeping. I studied hard and was pretty happy with my life until I walked in on Daddy and his lover, a fellow cop named Hugo, who had been like an uncle to me since I was a child. I was devastated. How could one of New York City's toughest and most decorated detectives turn out to be gay? Why hadn't he ever told me? Why had he lied to me for all those years? Worse, how could he string his girlfriend, Evelyn, along when he knew that she wanted to get married?

I moved out and went to live with Asha, swearing that I would never talk to my father or even look at his face again.

Asha talked me into letting him come to my wedding. He and I did the whole father/daughter dance thing but that was it.

We don't talk.

When Yero and I came back from our honeymoon, I didn't call Dad.

When Yero and I got this apartment in Harlem, I didn't call Dad.

When Asha got married, I didn't invite Dad and made her promise me that she wouldn't either.

Evelyn didn't come to my wedding or Asha's, but I am confident that she'll get in touch with me someday. We love each other. She just needs some space right now.

The good news is that I've finally landed a job. I refused to accept the money that Daddy offered to open my own boutique, but my work as an editorial assistant for a fashion magazine keeps me in the industry I love, even though it is a desk job and I don't meet the designers or stylists. Unfortunately, it also only pays fifteen thousand a year and our rent is two thousand a month. Yero and I are constantly juggling rent notices, utility bills, and subway fare and trying to cut down on food. We are living hand to mouth and it is very stressful. Maybe that is why Yero walks around looking so worried.

After babysitting a little girl to earn extra money and standing up in a packed subway car for almost half an hour, I was looking forward to a quiet apartment and a bowl of soup.

When I turned the corner of 135th Street, I saw that Yero was sitting on the stoop. Why was he sitting outside in this cold weather?

Yero is still the honest, caring, and helpful brother that I fell in love with during eleventh grade.

I walked faster, grabbed his cheeks, and kissed him on the lips. "Yero, why are you sitting out here?"

He smiled wearily. "My knees hurt, honey."

"Your knees? Did you fall or something?"

He shook his head, looking confused. "No."

"Yero, this is crazy. Come on. Get up and let's go upstairs."

He was in obvious pain as we walked the two flights up. One thing was clear. Yero needed to see a doctor. I told him so and he waved away the suggestion.

"I just need some vitamins, honey."

I opened the door and we entered our neat and tiny dwelling. As we took our coats off, I watched his face intently. "Is something bothering you, Yero?"

He pulled off his scarf and gloves. "Nothing but money, honey."

So that was it.

He sighed and stretched out on the couch as I lit a stick of cinnamon incense.

"What kind of soup do you want for dinner, Yero?"

"Soup? What else do we have?" he asked with a fake pout.

I smiled and stepped over his long legs. "We have spaghetti but no sauce. We have soup but no bread. We have rice but no meat."

Yero's strong, dark African features and thick locks had a commanding majesty, but his normally smooth forehead was now creased.

"Damn."

I sat down next to him and gave him a big hug.

"What was that for?"

"To stop you from worrying," I replied.

He stroked my face.

We kissed.

"I have thirty extra dollars," he said. "Let's have Chinese food."

"Okay. Do you want to go to the place around the corner?"

"Naw. My knees are killing me. Do you mind going out for it?"

"Yero, please call that therapist that I used to see."

"A shrink?"

"Yes. Please, Yero. I know you don't want to go, but do it for me?"

"Sure, baby, whatever you say."

By the time I came back with the food, he was sound asleep. I ate alone. I slept alone. Yero remained on the couch in his post office uniform. He didn't wake up till morning.

Chapter 3

PENELOPE

After presents have been opened, wrapping paper is discarded, and the ball has dropped in Times Square, the reality coach comes charging back in with credit card bills, bitter unromantic cold, and yesterday's problems as its ugly passengers. All poor people know this. Everyone over forty—both rich and poor—knows this. It is only the young, wealthy folks who get caught by surprise when their problems return in the coach wearing faces that are even harder and nastier than before.

That's just the way age works.

Since most of the thirty-five hundred people who lived in the town of Hercsville, Long Island, were both affluent and under forty, New Year's Day was a gloomy one.

Janice Webster, the sixty-five-year-old woman who some believed was distantly related to Hercsville's founder, was working from home on the first day of the year. Owner of the *Hercsville Democrat* and Hercsville Realty, she still had a newspaper to write and a HOME FOR SALE ad to design. A lifelong teetotaler, she peered out her closed bedroom window and made a loud humph, humph sound of disapproval. "Everybody in town got a hangover this morning. Stupid fools."

The temperature was near freezing, so the trees, already bereft of leaves, now wore dozens of tiny icicles that shimmered like

dangly crystal earrings. Brown-faced Santas still blinked red and
green on the lawns. The strings of Christmas lights had not yet
been removed from the windows, and green wreaths remained
on all the front doors.

Hercsville was still, cold, and pretty.

On Break Street, all of the shops were closed.

Just south of Break stood the imposing HCS Baptist Church.
While her mother, Janice Webster, was peering out the window,
Penelope Brewster arrived early to kneel and pray for the continued good health of herself and her own daughter, Thelma, and
to ask God for an end to Thelma's romance with Crenshaw Ellison.

Reverend Best was inside, hoping that some of the sinners who
had partied all last night would drop by. After all, it was Sunday
morning. He was in the mood to give one of his forty-five-minute
lectures about the fiery hell that awaited all the misguided souls
who refused to step into the Light.

He greeted Penelope with outstretched hands. "Good morning, Dr. Penny. Happy New Year!"

They exchanged kisses on the cheek.

"Thanks, Reverend. You don't have much of a crowd."

Reverend Best gazed ruefully around the church and smiled.
"Not yet. But they'll show up. I have faith."

Penelope yawned and started down the aisle toward the front
pews where she could kneel in peace. "Good luck."

Exactly thirty minutes later, Penelope left the church.
Reverend Best was still waiting and smiling.

A week later it was business as usual in Hercsville, which meant
that Dr. Penelope Brewster was not in a good mood.

The woman was unyielding on the subject of time, so even
though Crenshaw Ellison was only three minutes late, she was
thoroughly pissed.

"I bust my ass trying to keep these little hellions in good mental health, and there is no gratitude from their parents," she
fumed to her empty office.

The little hellions she was referring to ranged in age from five
to nineteen. Dr. Penny, as everyone called her, was a clinical psy-

chologist, specializing in children. Since she was the only mental health practitioner in town, an adult would occasionally stumble in, attend sessions for a couple of weeks, and then disappear. But her bread and butter were the troubled children of Hercsville. The wealthy, troubled children because Dr. Penny did not believe in freebies. After all, she reasoned, what would happen if she started treating people who couldn't afford to pay? She was a single parent herself and Thelma would soon be applying for college. Four years of college tuition . . . the very thought of it frightened her.

Thelma's father went to jail for embezzling a million dollars from his employer when Thelma was only six months old. She did not know what he looked like. Right after John Brewster's conviction and fifteen-year sentencing, Penelope had picked the child up and moved to Hercsville.

Penelope Brewster was a tall and statuesque brown-skinned woman with strong features and, reddish permed hair, which she wore in a loose pageboy. She had mapped out her life at an early age and would never forgive John Brewster for throwing her off course. John was a Moorehouse graduate. The two had married and set up housekeeping in the Atlanta suburb of Buckhead. There, the young psychologist and her CPA husband enjoyed a bright life with plenty of money, good friends, and then Thelma, a beautiful newborn who looked exactly like her mother.

After the trial, she could not go anywhere in Buckhead without enduring the stares, finger pointing, and not-so-subtle questions that always followed scandal.

So she called her mother, and Janice Webster had swung into action.

Janice informed the citizens of Hercsville that her daughter caught her husband cheating and immediately divorced him. She needed the townsfolk to give Penelope and her baby daughter, Thelma, a warm welcome and a permanent place in their hearts.

Penelope endured the welcome-home party that was held in her mother's luxurious home and used her savings to buy her own little house and set up her practice.

Five minutes late.

She went and stood beside the window, her arms crossed rigidly against her breasts, her chest heaving with disapproval. She saw them before they saw her.

Crenshaw Ellison walking hand in hand toward the office with her daughter, Thelma. They were laughing.

Stupid little chain snatcher, Penelope thought maliciously.

She loathed the Ellison family and charged them three times her normal rate. Each week she deposited the extra cash into Thelma's college fund.

Crenshaw Ellison was a short and puny sixteen-year-old with close-cropped hair, yellow skin like his father's, and lips that were far too thin. He looked like a scared twelve-year-old, and if he didn't have a crush on her precious daughter, Penny would have felt sorry for the boy.

His mother and father were both tall and big-boned. The father's worldwide reputation was too grand, the legend too big for the boy to ever measure up to. The mother was a fool.

Penny rattled the bracelets on her arms and watched in horror as Crenshaw Ellison gave Thelma a kiss on the lips. She took a step backward so that the kids wouldn't see her.

But she knew that something had to be done about that romance. And soon.

Her heels clicked across the parquet floor as she walked briskly toward the door. She waited. There was a knock. She took a deep breath, forced a smile onto her lips, and opened the door.

Crenshaw smiled back, looking up at her with his thin shoulders encased in a coat that probably cost more than her car.

"How are you today, Miss Penny?"

"Fine, Crenshaw. Why don't you have a seat? You're late but we do have some time left."

"I'm only five minutes late," Crenshaw said sadly.

She wanted to say *if you hadn't been so busy trying to get into my daughter's panties, you would have been on time,* but she didn't.

"I've told you time and again, Crenshaw, that time is money."

"I know."

"Good. Now, how are things going at home?"

He sighed and rolled his eyes at the ceiling. "Same. Mama still buggin' and Cheery startin' to sound just like her."

"How so?"

He mimicked the voice of a little girl. "I don't like it here. It's cold. People think they white. I wanna go home."

"And you? Do you want to go home, Crenshaw?"

Crenshaw looked her straight in the eye. "I wouldn't leave Thelma if my life depended on it."

Chapter 4

THELMA

Penelope and Thelma had a terrific relationship. Mother believed that her only child would continue on her virginal road to an Ivy League college, then law school, marry a rich/conservative black man, and live happily ever after. Thelma (who was already smoking marijuana and having sex with Crenshaw) planned to marry him right after high school, attend any college that would accept them both, and let the future take care of itself. Since Thelma was smart enough to keep her mouth shut, the two females coexisted peacefully in their modest house on Woodycrest Street.

Thelma Brewster turned off Break Street and made her way one block up Bronx Avenue to the space where she and Crenshaw had parked his Lexus. She was excited about the fact that tonight her mother was attending a town council meeting and then heading over to a seminar for black psychologists way over in Stonybrook, which was a couple of towns away. That meant she had four or five uninterrupted hours in front of her. At least four hours to spend in the Ellison household with Crenshaw's mother, Shareeka, his sister, Cheery, and of course, Crenshaw himself after the head-shrinking session was over. She hoped that Dayshawn was away on business, because Crenshaw always acted so mad and weird when his father was around.

She drove carefully, obeying all traffic signs and watching out for all the young people who, ecstatic to be out of school for the day, walked haphazardly in front of the pretty silver car. The road was icy but Crenshaw had told her not to be afraid of the inclement weather. "Just respect it" was what he said. She smiled. He was the only man she would ever love and they had already decided to get married right after high school. They would drive into Manhattan and get married at city hall before anyone could stop them. If their parents insisted they go to college after that, so be it. They would go to any campus, study any subject, and endure any campus rules. As long as they were a married couple.

Once their decision had been made, a quiet peace would settle over their relationship.

In front of her mother, Thelma still pretended to be the shy, studious teenager who was unsure of herself in the face of her mother's confidence. But alone with Crenshaw she was a young woman with a big secret and big plans.

It felt good.

Thelma drove around the Sedgewick Circle and past the residence that supposedly once belonged to Kool D.J. Herc, the town's alleged founder. It was Janice Webster's place now.

Like most Hercsville natives, she hated Janice and her mean, spiteful little newspaper. Even though Janice was her grandmother and she knew it was childish, Thelma stuck her tongue out at the residence as she drove past. The newspaper wasn't Thelma's only reason for despising the shrewd old woman. Grandma Janice Webster had never been the cuddly, nurturing, grandmotherly type that appeared in storybooks wearing an apron and baking cookies. Instead, Janice constantly reminded her that her father was a thief and that she had his genes. Therefore, she should watch her every step and guard against her terrible biologically directed inclination to engage in deceit.

Crenshaw's mother opened the door wearing a gold brocade lounging outfit and matching slippers. Shareeka's weaved and dyed blond hair was not hanging to her waist like it usually did. Instead, she had brushed it up into a gelled pile on the top of her head. Enormous hoops dangled from her ears. She reached out to pull Thelma inside, and the young girl was amazed that each ten-inch nail on her slender hands was decorated in a gold swirly pattern that matched the lounging outfit. Her face was carefully made up, complete with shiny gold lipstick and false eyelashes. But the eyes, usually sad and dim, were sparkling.

"Come on in, gurl!"

Excitement crackled in the air around her. It was infectious and Thelma found herself grinning before the door slammed behind her.

"What's going on?"

"Gurl, Shareeka has got herself a plan!"

Chapter 5

NANCY

Nancy Rosa St. Bart was dreaming when a shrill ring of the telephone on her nightstand jolted her awake. She didn't want to let go of the dream. In it, she was a guest at the wedding reception of Denzel Washington and Pauletta Pearson. Although Pauletta looked fetching in her bridal gown, no one was paying her any attention.

Instead, the groom and all of his very rich male friends were singing the name "Nancy." They were captivated by her gorgeous face and stunning figure. They were throwing diamonds and thousand-dollar bills at her feet as they wept and begged for her hand in marriage.

"Bruce, answer the phone," she murmured. Then she remembered that her boyfriend, a struggling stand-up comedian, was out of town.

Nancy moaned and opened her eyes. The numbers on the digital clock showed that it was a quarter to four in the morning. Someone must be sick or dead. Her heart began to race as she picked up the receiver.

"Hello?"

"Is this Nancy?" It was a female voice. One that she'd heard before but could not place.

"Yes?"

"Nancy," the woman said, "I saw your picture in *Essence*. You look good."

"Who is this?"

"I bet you make a whole lotta money, don't you, Nancy?"

"I'm going to hang up."

"Don't. Bruce ain't there to protect you tonight."

"Who are you?"

"A friend. We are still friends, aren't we, Nancy?"

"I don't have any friends who call me at four in the fucking morning on a weeknight. If you're some woman who is fooling around with Bruce, take him and be happy."

"I need some money."

"Lady, you sure dialed the wrong number. Go find somebody else to bother. I've got to get up in three hours."

"You owe a debt, Nancy, and it must be paid."

"What? What debt are you talking about?"

The female voice became threatening. "You lousy, stinking bitch. I could have had a life like yours."

Nancy's mouth went dry, her hands began to shake, and her eyes darted around the corners of her bedroom as though she was looking for an intruder in the shadows.

"Who is this?"

"You figure out who I am. If you don't, I will kill everyone that you care about, starting with your cowardly mother and that dumb-ass brother of yours."

Nancy slammed the receiver back down in its cradle and turned on both lamps.

The sheet, blanket, and comforter suddenly seemed too confining. Nancy pushed them away and sat up. She realized that it would be impossible for her to rest peacefully. She pulled at the silk scarf that covered her head. It felt too tight. She rubbed her eyes until they began to sting. Her heart was still racing and she bent forward, placing her head between her knees. Breathe in. Breathe out. Breathe in. Breathe out.

She was glad that Bruce was out of town. The incident would

have reminded him of the affair she'd had with a married man two years ago. Somehow the wife had gotten hold of her number and harassed them for weeks. Bruce would have sighed deeply and said something like "I won't go through this again, Nancy." She would have argued, insisting that she was not involved in anything that would have triggered a hostile telephone call. He would not have believed her. How could he? She'd lied through her teeth two years ago and, at first, her act had been very convincing.

Nancy decided that she would not tell Bruce about the disturbing phone call. She would have the phone number changed and tell Bruce that too many fans had somehow found it on the Internet.

Nancy felt calmer.

She and Bruce were the same age—thirty-nine—and the same astrological sign—Scorpio. They also wanted the same things out of life—fame and boatloads of money. Although she was not a big star, she was a regular on one of the country's most popular soap operas. The caller was probably just some nutty fan. But the caller had mentioned her family. The caller said her mother was a coward and her brother a dumb-ass. Both statements were true, but how would one of her fans know that? Nancy never discussed her personal life with anyone.

Maybe the woman would call back and drop some useful clues. She stared at the phone, willing it to ring so she could clear up the mystery, but nothing happened.

She swung her bare feet onto the carpeted floor. The caller had asked her to play some stupid game. What an insane request. She didn't have time for that kind of nonsense. Even if she did, there was no way she'd spend it to save her mother and brother. The two of them weren't worth the price of a damned postage stamp. She went into the living room, sat down on the sofa, and wrung her hands.

Maybe the call had just been a cruel joke, a monstrous hoax perpetrated by some jealous family member.

The thought made her feel better. She used the remote control to turn on the TV. She would watch the early morning news shows until it was time to get dressed for work.

Nancy fell asleep on the sofa. This time she dreamt of her brother, Randall. He was wearing a blue Cub Scout uniform. He was only eight and the cutest little boy on the block. There was no sign of the prematurely bald, third-rate burglar that he would become. He was pulling at her hand, trying to get her to follow him. She was resisting for some reason and they tugged back and forth for a moment. Then he let go and she fell off a cliff. When she landed in the ocean, the water somehow created a ringing sound in her ears. The sound was annoying enough to wake her up.

The ringing sound was actually the telephone.

There was no extension in the living room, which meant she had a choice. Go back upstairs into the bedroom and pick up the receiver or make a right turn into the kitchen and answer it there. She chose the kitchen with its yellow wall phone.

"Hello?"

"Is this Nancy?" It was the same voice.

"Yes."

"Nancy," the woman said, "why did you hang up on me?"

"Because I have no intention of doing what you ask."

"I didn't ask you to do anything, Nancy."

"Yes, you did."

"I didn't ask you for anything. I simply told you my plans and gave you a choice."

"Well, I choose not to participate and if you want to kill Mama and Randall, go right ahead. You'll be doing them both a favor."

The caller laughed and Nancy recognized the sound.

"Tough talk. Well, you just made things a lot easier for me, Miss Smartypants."

"What does that mean?"

"It means the old rules are out the window. I'm going to let your mama and Randall live. Here are the new rules. If you can figure out my identity and the reason why I hate you, I'll let you live also. If you can't, I will kill you and Bruce."

Nancy's hands started to shake. "Why are you doing this to me?"

"Because you had a chance to save me and you didn't."

"Save you from what?"

"I don't have time to stroll down memory lane with you, bitch. If you don't deliver, I will riddle your fat, double-crossing ass with bullets. Are we clear?"

The caller hung up before she could answer.

Nancy stumbled into one of her three bathrooms and gripped the edge of the sink until her teeth stopped chattering. Then she started her morning ritual: wash hands exactly sixteen times and rinse thirty-two times, wash face with special oatmeal scrub, brush teeth, shower, and towel off, slather skin with cocoa butter, wrap body in towel, and get dressed in bedroom.

As always, her hair and makeup took nearly an hour, but the results were worth every second of the time spent.

What to wear? She needed an outfit that made her feel powerful and in control.

She chose a navy blue skirt suit, a white silk blouse, and black pumps. She had an early morning breakfast with her agent before reporting to the set. The meeting was about money . . . about how she was going to fire him if he didn't get her some movie roles . . . about how sick she was of the soap opera. The meeting would be quick and to the point. She had to be on the set of *The Bridesmaid* by 10:00 a.m.

Nancy was a short, heavyset woman with thick, glossy black hair that fell below her shoulders, dark chocolate skin, and slanty eyes framed with long lashes. She was a beautiful woman who took great pride in the fact that the hair on her head was neither sewn nor glued in. Young, whippet-thin ladies who tossed their hair weaves around made her sick. Unfortunately, the director had a number of them in the cast and crew, which caused Nancy to roll her eyes in disgust several times a day.

A final once-over in the bathroom's full-length mirror: Her skin was flawless and the expertly applied foundation, eyeliner, mascara, and lipstick showed off her high cheekbones and pouty lips. Her hair, now freed from the wire rollers, bounced slightly below her shoulders.

She turned this way and that, trying to find some fault with her appearance, but the suit fit perfectly. She smiled in satisfaction, decided to ignore the crazed fan who kept calling, and walked out the front door.

Chapter 6

SHAREEKA

"Shit!"

Thelma looked up from her homework. "What's the matter?"

Shareeka, who was sitting at the kitchen table across from her young guest, slammed her cell phone shut. "I've tried two different numbers for this dude named Push, and both of them are disconnected."

"Who is he and why does he call himself Push?"

His real name was Calvin Points, but women in the Crenshaw section of Los Angeles had nicknamed him Push long ago because he thrust so hard during sexual intercourse. Shareeka did not think the information was appropriate to share with Thelma. "He is a very aggressive person."

"Oh."

"Push is one of Dayshawn's oldest and dearest friends. There is no way I can give a party and leave him out."

The party. It was the only thing on Shareeka's mind. The party was her latest scheme, designed to make Dayshawn nostalgic for California so they could move back West to the land of sunshine and palm trees.

She hated New York.

She hated Long Island and she hated Hercsville.

But most of all, she hated Dayshawn, the movie producer. When they married, right out of high school, he had been the lead rapper in a gangsta rap group called The Gangbangers, and everyone called him Bustacap. The group had broken up long ago and he made a living by producing, directing, and acting in corny movies designed to appeal to midwestern white folks.

Shareeka wanted their old life back.

"Seems to me like Mr. Ellison is on some new shit now. Maybe he doesn't want to see Push anymore."

Shareeka could not see that a child had opened its mouth and spoken a truth that she needed to hear. "New shit? That's street talk, Thelma. Where did you hear something like that?"

"Crenshaw."

"Oh. Well. Crenshaw comes from a place where that kind of talk is okay. That's why I like y'all goin' together. You and your mama can show him a different way to do things. Don't pick up bad habits from him. Make him learn good habits from you. Okay?"

"But I like it when Crenshaw talks like that," Thelma protested. "He sounds just like the cute guys on the BET videos."

Shareeka opened her mouth to reply and then decided against it. Thelma was a good, old-fashioned girl. She was just going through a phase.

"Shareeka?"

"What?"

"What are you going to do if this plan doesn't work? My mother says that a woman always has to have a plan B because men are so unpredictable."

Shareeka's chest tightened. She stood up and looked out of the window. "I don't know, Thelma. But I'll think of something."

"Shareeka?"

"What?"

"If your parents and sisters moved to the East Coast, would you like it here? Is it just that you miss them?"

Shareeka closed her eyes and remembered a recent party that she and her husband had attended. It had been an elegant bash out in Southampton with a guest list that included Nicole Kidman,

Jennifer Aniston, John Travolta, Calvin Klein, and a whole bunch of models and fashion designers. Dayshawn had been the only black male on the premises and he was so proud of that fact, it made Shareeka sick. He spoke slowly and enunciated each word so hard that he almost sounded like a man with a bad, fake-ass British accent. This was the world that Dayshawn moved in now. He was trying to be someone that he wasn't.

"No. I don't want my family or Dayshawn's family to move here. I want to go home. I mean, California is movie country. Wouldn't it be easier to live on the West Coast than here in the cold and this fucked-up snow?"

"There's your plan B," Thelma said calmly.

Shareeka turned to look at the pretty, solidly built teen with the reddish complexion and short, curly brown hair. "How you figure?"

"Tell Mr. Ellison that if he moves back to California and starts hanging with the big-shot movie people, then he will get an Oscar for one of his movies. Then he'll really have the respect that he wants."

For a moment, Shareeka wondered how Crenshaw's girlfriend might be manipulating him. "Go ahead."

"That's all. My mother says that to get somebody to do something, you have to appeal to their own self-interest and not tell them what you're getting out of it."

Shareeka made a mental note to have a long, long talk with her son.

Chapter 7

ASHA

I slipped into a white Dolce & Gabbana tuxedo blouse and a pair of butterfly embroidered jeans with a fuchsia ponyhair patch that had a gold-tone logo on the back pocket. I pulled a pair of black Prada Linea Rossa boots up my legs and I was dressed. I figured that I'd just put on a little lipstick and wear a ponytail. We were going to pay Saundra a visit before hitting a new and casual club down in Greenwich Village.

Nick ambled into our bedroom, buck naked and sipping from a coffee mug. He sat his ass down on my pink, cushy vanity stool. Was he trying to start an argument?

"You look nice, honey."

I gave him a sweet smile and blew him a kiss.

"Tell you what." He grinned. "Why don't we just get some champagne and stay home?"

"Saundra and Yero have probably been cooking all day for us. Besides, I have to get out of this house before I explode."

Nick sighed. "I hardly get a chance to enjoy our new home."

"Yeah, well, I'm here all day with nothing to do."

"Nobody told you to quit your job."

He was right about that. It's just that I started working so young that I jumped at the first chance I'd ever had to become a lady of leisure. It had been a stupid move. Not only had I put my career on stall but I didn't even have a hobby that would keep me busy.

"Nick, could you please put your clothes on."

"What should I wear?"

"What?"

"You said that we should dress down so that Saundra and Yero don't think we're trying to flash like we're rich. I don't know what that means. So go through my closet and tell me what to wear that will make me look like a poor man who just happens to drive a Mercedes."

He was smiling.

I had to laugh. "Did I really say that?"

"Yes, you did."

I threw a lipstick at him playfully and he ducked.

"Wear what you want."

I stood back to admire myself in the mirror. "Nick?"

"What?"

"Do you know how lucky you are?"

"Because you're so fine?"

"Yes."

"Yes, Asha. I know how lucky I am."

He walked over and stood behind me. His hands cupped my breasts as we both watched in the mirror.

"Nick!"

He stopped feeling me up and stepped back. "Okay. I'm going to throw on some black jeans and a turtleneck. Is that all right with you?"

"Okay."

We pulled out of the driveway half an hour later.

"So, what's up with Yero?" he asked.

"What do you mean?"

"I heard you and Saundra on the phone talking the other night. Is he sick or something?"

"Saundra thinks that he might be depressed, Mr. Nosy."

"Shit, if I had to eat all that fucking rabbit food that Saundra puts in front of a brother, I'd be depressed too."

"Yero is a vegan just like my sister is."

We both looked at each other in horror. What the fuck would my sister be serving tonight?

"Let's take them a whole pizza," Nick suggested.

"That would be rude."

"Why? People bring wine when they're invited to dinner. Sometimes they even bring a whole cake for dessert."

"Yeah," I replied, "but they don't show up with the actual dinner."

"Well then, let's stop somewhere and grab a bite. I'm not sitting there half-starved all night."

"McDonald's?"

"Cool," he said.

Saundra stood in the doorway of her apartment. The sounds of classical music and what sounded like wind chimes came from behind her. The smells of spaghetti sauce and garlic wafted over her shoulder. She was wearing a yellow cotton wraparound skirt and a yellow tube top. Her locks were oiled and hung almost to her breasts. Her feet were bare. There were bracelets on her wrists and ankles.

I kissed her on the cheeks and hugged her tight. "Saundra, it is wintertime. Why are you dressed for the beach?"

She let go of me and grabbed Nick. "Hi, brother-in-law."

He responded with a grin and a pull on one of her locks.

She said, "It is cold outside, Asha, but there is sunshine in the home of Mr. and Mrs. Brown. That is why I'm dressed in yellow."

Whatever.

Their place was dinky. It reminded me a whole lot of the apartment that Mama, Saundra, and I once shared.

Did Saundra see it too?

Right off the entryway was a kitchen with jacked-up tile floors and an old-fashioned sink that showed the pipe sliding up the wall toward the ceiling. To the left of the entryway was a bedroom with no door to close. Saundra had wisely converted that space, which was only big enough for a four-year-old with a small amount of toys, into a storage room/mini-library. In back of that was the bathroom that had a tub so old that it actually stood on four feet that looked like claws. Straight ahead was the living room, where Yero reclined on a brightly colored sofa staring at some romantic drama on BET.

Every room was shiny, spotless, and painted either yellow or red. Every room was furnished. The décor was late 1960s white hippie. But that was Saundra. She was born to live among love beads, Lava Lamps, beanbag chairs, ceramic kitchenware, and blond wood tables painted blue. It was like living inside a roll of LifeSavers.

I shuddered involuntarily and then checked myself as Yero rose to greet us.

I studied him closely. He did look depressed, but who wouldn't be in his situation? He worked at the post office selling stamps and money orders all day, then came home to a veggie burger or homemade soup created by a smiling Saundra. She told me that they meditated each night before going to bed. On the weekend, he dealt with his out-of-control, hoodlum younger brother and the rest of his dysfunctional, biological family. If I were Yero, I'd either run away or kill myself.

At one time, they had a serious problem in their relationship and Saundra called off their engagement. She showed up on my doorstep in the middle of the night and I let her stay with me. It was horrible. My refrigerator was packed with veggie patties, soy milk, fake cheese, and some kind of nutty, crunchy bread that looked like it was made of dying tree bark. She listened to either elevator music or some eerie sounds that sounded like prisoners whispering through a steel plate. There was no point in my complaining, because she would either give me a lecture about negative energy, try to force me into taking up yoga, or just smile at me like some demented moonie.

Don't get me wrong. I loved my only sibling, but if Yero Brown was depressed, I could definitely dig it.

We did the usual chitchat thing and then Saundra served mugs of delicious homemade apple cider. Nick and I sat at the wooden table hoping that she would serve something light for dinner. We had gone through a drive-through Mickey D's and were stuffed with burgers and fries.

Luck was with us. Dinner was some kind of tuna dish made with fake mayonnaise, carrots, and celery served with apples and pita bread. We were able to eat enough to make Saundra happy.

"So," she asked, "why are you guys all dressed up?"

"We're going to a club when we leave here."

Nick groaned. "If it was up to me, I'd go back home and watch a good movie. But Miss Party-Till-I'm-Forty insists that we go shake our asses to some music."

No, he did not!

"First of all, I'm just past my twenty-sixth birthday and it is bad enough that thirty is close to kicking me in the ass and I haven't accomplished anything yet without you making smart remarks. Secondly, I'm at home all the time watching movies while you travel around the country. Plus, if you didn't want to go dancing tonight, all you had to do was say so."

"Chill," Yero said. "I think Nick is just stuffed with good food and enjoying good company. He doesn't want to break his groove."

I glared at Nick, who glared back.

"Just say so? You would have had a fit, Asha! And I'm tired of hearing about how you're home all day. You sound like some housewife out of the 1950s. Nobody is stopping you from getting a job or going back to school. Just get out of the house Monday morning and find something to do."

The fact that he was absolutely right pissed me off even more. "Fine. I will. And, for your information, I don't want to dance with you tonight. I'll go by my damned self."

Saundra held out a hand to me. "Asha, please stop."

She was right. It wasn't her fault that my lifelong dream of sitting on my ass while a wealthy man went out every morning to support me had turned out to be a gigantic drag. It wasn't Yero's fault and it wasn't Nick's fault, either.

My smile was sweet and contrite. "I'm sorry."

Nick should have left it at that but he didn't.

"You should be sorry, Asha. When I leave here, I'm going home and get some rest. I'm sick of your shit. Do what you want."

He picked up a slice of pita bread, smeared the tuna concoction on it, stuffed the whole thing in his mouth, and turned his back to me and started talking directly to Yero.

Fuck him.

I got up without another word, kissed my sister on the cheek, and held out my hand. "Give me the car keys."

Nick sighed. "Cut the drama. You're used to driving around city streets. Not over bridges and under tunnels. What are you try-ing to prove?"

I just stood there with my hand out.

Saundra got up too. "Asha, this is crazy. You cannot go through the tunnel and on to the highway in the middle of the night just to prove some ridiculous point. You could kill someone."

"The only one I'm ready to kill is Nick," I said through gritted teeth.

He threw the keys into my hand and I was out the door.

One of my old lovers was a guy named Brent. He used to drive like he was trying to win a medal for safest driver of the year. I put the car in gear and drove carefully like Brent. I was no longer in the mood to dance, but I didn't want to spend the next six months in some intensive care unit just because my plans had fallen through.

Nick used to be a real romantic. I mean a writing poetry, bring-ing flowers, giving kisses, holding hands, and always ready to fuck kind of guy. Ever since we got married, he has been a drag. He ac-tually had the nerve to tell me that now that I was married, it was time for me to act like a lady. That was on the first night of our honeymoon. I thought it was a joke, but ever since we moved out to the suburbs, he has been trying to turn me into a mini version of his mother. That shit just ain't gonna work.

I stuck to the speed limit and made it through the Queens Midtown Tunnel without incident.

Chapter 8

SAUNDRA

I feel sorry for Nick. He loves Asha to death and tries very hard to make her happy. He even went up against his own family when she refused to sign a prenuptial agreement before their wedding. Apparently, all the women who marry into the Seabrook family are forced to sign prenups. But not my sister. I have to say that I don't blame her for that. But they were really shocked. There are not many women from our background who will walk away from the chance of marrying a wealthy guy. But Asha told them that she was willing to do just that and she wasn't playing. Nick was desperate. He got his way by threatening to leave the family business. Since he is an only child, that really upset the parental apple cart.

He wants her to become a society lady. The kind of upper-class black woman who gives dinner parties, hosts debutante balls, gets involved with the Jack and Jill organization, and serves on a dozen committees.

She wants Nick to give her an unlimited amount of money to decorate their new house, an open checkbook for a fabulous wardrobe, and a baby to secure her access to the Seabrook fortune. Then she wants him to get lost.

Of course, Asha never actually came out and told me that she will ditch Nick after they have a baby. But I'm not stupid. She is not in love with Nick. Marriage is hard and Asha is not the most patient person in the world. So I just put two and two together: Marriage is hard and Asha doesn't have enough feelings for him to go the distance.

Some people grow up poor and learn to live with that fact from their past. Others spend the rest of their lives grubbing for money, and no matter how fat their bank accounts get, they will never feel that enough is enough. Asha is one of those people who aches for financial security but will never know when she has found it.

I feel sorry for her.

I feel sorry for Nick.

I hope that I'm wrong about the baby part. I'd love to become an auntie, but what child deserves to be born into some shit like this?

I told Nick that I'd leave him and Yero alone to do some male bonding.

Nick asked Yero, "Feel like doing some serious drinking, man?"

"Maybe a nonalcoholic beer or two," Yero answered.

Nick frowned. "That ain't drinking."

"Yero hasn't been feeling well," I said.

Nick shrugged. "Well, my wife has walked out on me, so you drink the beer and I'll drown my sorrows in something stronger."

I stood up. "You two lovebirds will be cooing at each other before sunrise."

Nick sighed. "You're probably right, but how long will the peace last? A week? Two weeks?"

I went around the kitchen table and kissed Nick good night. "Maybe you should spend the night. Friends don't let friends drive drunk."

The two men groaned at my corny truth.

"Yero, the phone number for the liquor store is in my desk. You two have fun!"

I left them talking guy talk and went to bed.

Chapter 9

SHAREEKA

Shareeka Grant was born in Compton, California, thirty-three years before. She was the youngest in a family of seven children—five girls and two boys. Her earliest memory was of Calvin Points's mother, who used to be her babysitter. Mother Points, as she was called, was a hard, cold woman who did not like children. She had given birth to Calvin because by the time she learned she was pregnant, it was too late for an abortion. She babysat the neighborhood children for extra money to supplement her welfare check. Mother Points did not keep any child that she was not allowed to hit. And she hit for the slightest infraction. One time, she accused six-year-old Shareeka of picking up a phone extension to listen in on her conversation. She slapped Shareeka hard across the face. "When I grow up, I'm gonna kick your ass for that," Shareeka said, weeping. Mother Points could not believe the child's audacity. It earned Shareeka a whole series of slaps, kicks, and punches.

Every morning, Shareeka and Calvin walked to school together. Although the advent of gangster rap music would put their neighborhood on the map as a violent, hopeless wasteland, that was far into the future. In the meantime, she and Calvin daydreamed, shared candy and bubblegum, and punched each other playfully on the arm as they ducked the crackheads who would grab a child's book bag to steal the contents. The crack whores were worse than their male counterparts. A male crackhead just wanted the schoolbag and any jewelry you were wearing. The females demanded shoes and hair barrettes that they could take home to their own kids to ease their already rickety consciences.

Calvin's nickname as a kid was Mack because he loved any kind of food that came out of McDonald's. That suited Mother Points just fine because she hated to cook more than she hated kids.

Since Shareeka's siblings were a lot older and mostly living elsewhere with kids of their own, she and Calvin were like brother and sister. They did everything together: bike riding, stone throwing, stealing candy from a local, overcrowded store. The only thing they disagreed on was music. Calvin hated rap music. He had an old, battered radio that was once owned by the father he couldn't remember. It was so dented that it could not get anything but the country-and-western station, and even then, only up to number 3 on the volume knob. So Calvin used to lie in bed with an old transister radio up to his ear listening to the fiddling and twanging sounds that came out of another region. Calvin loved country music, and Shareeka kept his secret. For he would surely have gotten his ass thoroughly kicked if she'd informed anyone else on the block.

By the time they were in seventh grade, Shareeka's favorite group was The Fat Boys and she had a gigantic crush on Markie D. This amused Calvin to no end.

"How you gonna fall in love with that big, fat Puerto Rican greasy, fur-hat-wearing muthafucka?" he asked.

They were sitting at a McDonald's sharing a nine-piece Chicken McNuggets and a strawberry shake.

"I like him cuz he light-skinned."

"That's really stupid."

Shareeka shrugged. "No more stupid than you listening to that Ku Klux Klan music."

Calvin flushed and changed the subject. "I think Puerto Ricans are just like Mexicans."

Shareeka shook her head. "They the same cuz they speak

Spanish and eat rice and beans a lot, but Puerto Ricans are classier. It's like they cousins and shit, but one got more money and stuff."

Calvin laughed. "Bullshit. You just saying that cuz you wanna give it up to Markie D."

Their friendship changed when Shareeka's mother hit the number for ten thousand dollars and decided to move. The move was only three blocks away, but it meant that the two youngsters were no longer living right next door to each other. A small thing but significant in the world of youngsters. Shareeka's new home was another rented house, but this one didn't have a leaky roof or unsafe stairs. It also had an extra bedroom that Shareeka could call her own. The street also had something else that made her happy. A chubby, brown-skinned boy with penetrating eyes. His name was Dayshawn Ellison and he wanted to be a rapper more than anything else in the world. He was out on the corner with a group of guys every night, rain or shine, hollering into an empty soda bottle that he pretended was a mic.

Shareeka did some investigating and discovered that he had a mother and father in his house, plus an older brother who was a cop. No wonder he was allowed to make all that damn noise in the street every day. Nobody wanted to fuck with a cop's kid brother.

When Shareeka took Calvin to sneak a glimpse at the would-be entertainer, Calvin snickered. "What the hell is wit you and these fat guys?"

Shareeka hadn't made the connection between Markie D and Dayshawn Ellison. It made her stop and think for a moment, but then she just shoved Calvin in the chest. "I want you to make friends with him so I can hang out wit y'all."

"Come on, girl. Why don't you just go over there and talk to his little fat ass?"

Calvin sounded jealous and a shadow crossed his face.

"No, it will make me look desperate."

"But you are desperate."

"Calvin, please," Shareeka whined.

And that's how the two neighborhood guys became homeboys for real. Three years went by and the trio was ready for high school. Dayshawn, who had started calling himself Bustacap, was still chunky but he had a gorgeous smile and curly black hair. He was handsome and knew it. Shareeka had taken the friend thing long enough. One night she made her move. It was a bold, brazen move. She came up behind him in Calvin's kitchen and held him around the waist as one slender hand slid down in his pants.

He turned around and kissed her hard on the mouth. They had been lovers ever since. Of course, if Mother Points had come through that door, their young lives would have ended right then and there.

A few years later, Calvin had become the neighborhood sex machine and everyone stopped calling him Mack and started calling him Push.

Now Shareeka was on the phone begging Push to come to the surprise "hood" party that she was throwing for her husband.

"Come on, Push, I'm paying for airfare, hotel, limos, everything. What is the big problem?"

"If he knew about this shit, it would be different, Shareeka. But I'm telling you, Dayshawn ain't gonna like this one bit and I ain't gonna get embarrassed in front of all those people. He don't wanna see me."

Something bad had gone down between Dayshawn and Calvin. Something bad enough to break up The Gangbangers and stop the two men from speaking to each other at all. Neither one of them had ever shared the secret with her.

"Look, Push. Whatever went down between y'all is way over. I mean, come on, it's been a good ten fucking years. Get over it."

"It ain't that simple, Shareeka."

Shareeka's temper flared. "Fine, muthafucka. Everybody else said they'll be here. I'm gonna tell Dayshawn that yo ass refused to come because you hate his goddamn ass. Okay?"

"Don't do that, Shareeka."

"Why not?"

"Because it's gonna set off some real bad shit if Dayshawn thinks I hate him. Some real bad shit. I'm telling you. Somebody is gonna get hurt and I'm not gonna let it be me."

"Tell me what happened," Shareeka whined desperately. "Tell me or I'll do it and I don't care who the fuck gets hurt."

"I can't tell you on the phone, Shareeka."

"You're just jerking my fucking chain, Push. I'm hanging the fuck up."

"Wait!"

"Are you gonna tell me?"

"No."

"Fine. I'm gonna tell Dayshawn that you told me the big fucking secret and that you said all of it was his fault."

Push actually moaned. "No. No."

"Damn!"

"You would do all this just for me to come to a party? Why, Shareeka?"

"Okay, I'll tell you the truth. I figure if Dayshawn sees all our old homies, he'll see that we don't belong here. I hate New York. I want to come home. Maybe the party will make him see that he wants to come home too."

"You just don't get it, do you?"

"Get what?"

He sighed. "Nothing. I'll be there, okay? But listen to me, Shareeka. If you hate New York, go somewhere else. Don't encourage Dayshawn to come back to Los Angeles. Try San Diego or some shit."

"Why?"

"Too many bad memories for him out here."

"Puhleeze, Calvin. Ain't nothin' really bad ever happen to Dayshawn. What are you talkin' about?"

"Forget it. You're giving a party and I'll be there."

Two hours later, she was eating lustily from a bowl of fried shrimp, sprinkled with hot sauce, sipping one ice-cold beer after another, and watching old music videos from way back when The Gangbangers was the biggest rap group in the world. Push, Spark, Bustacap, and Gat. They were really riding high back then. Now Push was broke, Spark ran a recording studio, no one dared call her husband by the nickname Bustacap anymore, and Gat had died of AIDS.

Cheery, her ten-year-old daughter, entered the room and stared at her father, rapping and cursing at the top of his lungs on the sixty-four-inch screen.

"Why don't Daddy sing anymore?"

"Because he is a movie director now," Shareeka snorted. "And don't tell him that I was watching these videos. I don't want to hear his mouth."

Cheery nodded obediently, her short braids standing at attention. "Can I have some ice cream?"

Shareeka, who was perched on the edge of the sofa in a lime-green lounging outfit, eyed her suspiciously. "Didn't you already have a pint of ice cream tonight? In fact, why ain't you in bed? It's almost eleven o'clock."

"But there's no school tomorrow. It's Friday night."

"I don't care. Little girls should be in bed."

"Can I?"

Shareeka waved a hand. "Go ahead. But then go to bed."

Cheery started to leave and then turned on her heel. "Mama?"

Shareeka didn't try to hide her irritation as she turned away from The Gangbangers again. "What?"

"Crenshaw said he needs you to pick him up. His girlfriend's car broke down."

"When did he call?"

"Just a minute ago."

"Why didn't you tell me?"

"We was talkin' about the ice cream."

Shareeka stood up and licked hot sauce off her fingers. "Where is that fool?"

"At Thelma's house."

"I didn't hear the phone ring."

"He called me on my cell," Cheery replied. "I guess he didn't want you to yell at him." She paused. "Just like you don't want to hear Daddy's mouth."

Shareeka fixed her with an evil stare. "Get the ice cream. Get upstairs. Call Crenshaw back and tell him to listen for my car horn. Don't move out of your room until I get back. Understand?"

Cheery nodded and skipped away.

Shareeka threw her overcoat over the lounging outfit and thrust her bare feet into a pair of galoshes that belonged to her husband. Penelope and Thelma Brewster lived less than five minutes away. She'd be back before her shrimp got cold.

It was freezing outside and she shivered on her way to the custombuilt, hot pink Lexus that Dayshawn had given her for Christmas. She backed out of the driveway and sailed along for two blocks, took a right turn, and then a car appeared in front of her. The driver seemed confused. The vehicle veered one way and then another.

Shareeka swerved her car to avoid a collision, but she didn't do it soon enough.

There was a loud bang, a screech of tires, and then the sound of spinning wheels and a car horn.

She watched as the driver, a short, slim woman, leaped out of her car.

Shareeka got out too, fully prepared to curse the stupid, reckless bitch completely out. But the woman was in tears. She was also shaking uncontrollably. Maybe she was an epileptic.

Shareeka grabbed her by the shoulders. "What's your name? Are you all right?"

The woman's mouth opened but nothing came out.

"It's okay. Nobody is hurt. Calm down. Do you live around here?"

The woman nodded.

"Where?"

But the woman just stood there shaking. Her eyes were big and wide. They widened even more when she noticed the damage to their cars. "Nick is going to kill me!" she wailed.

Shareeka felt better. At least the woman was talking.

"Who is Nick?"

"My husband!"

"Oh, fuck that, gurl. His ass should just be glad that you didn't get hurt."

The woman smiled.

Shareeka took a good look at her. She had flawless cream skin with a slight red undertone. She was short . . . about five-feet-two. Her Siamese-shaped eyes were hazel.

"You're right."

"Good. I ran out of the house without my stuff, but if you give me your phone number, I'll call you tomorrow to do all the insurance stuff."

The woman started crying again.

Shareeka remembered her shrimp. The hot sauce. The stack of DVDs featuring her husband, Bustacap, when he was the lead rapper of the world-famous Gangbangers.

"Lady, what is your problem?"

"I lost control of the car."

"No shit. What are you doing out on the road?"

"I'm sorry about your car. I can't get back behind the wheel tonight."

"Listen, I don't have time for this. What is your name?"

"Asha."

"Well, Asha, I'm Shareeka. My little girl is home alone and my boy is waiting for me to pick him up. I gotta go."

"Could you drive me home? I live right here in Hercsville."

Jesus! Why couldn't she have one evening of peace?

"Okay. I'm only doin' this so you don't kill somebody's chile out here tonight. I'm going to park your car by the road. Then you'll have to come along with me while we pick up Crenshaw. Once I get him in the car, I'll drop you off home. Hurry up!"

Chapter 10

PENELOPE

Penelope allowed Thelma to serve her guest a snack of chips, onion dip, cookies, and juice but dared the young girl to go up in the refrigerator and start frying up her real food. She then went to her room and tried to watch television but found herself drawn more and more to the top of the staircase in an effort to hear what Thelma and Crenshaw were saying down in the sunken living room.

Jesus! Thelma must be kissing that barely-out-of-the-ghetto little fool, she thought in dismay at one point when the laughter and voices stopped downstairs. What on earth had got into her wholesome, squeaky-clean kid? She rushed back to her room, pulled the nightgown off, and slipped naked into a T-shirt and a pair of jeans. *I'll just march right up to the sofa and snatch that little creep up by the back of his neck and physically toss his little ass right out of my house,* she thought.

But when she was halfway down the stairs, she heard the two of them laughing. She stood there, unsure what to do next and remembering what her own behavior had been like at sixteen.

Janice Webster had been a by-the-book type of mother. When Penelope was young, all the woman's sentences had started with the same two words: nice young. Nice young girls did not stay out after dark. Nice young girls did not dance with their bodies pressed close to boys. Nice young girls did not even think about having sex before they got married. Nice young girls did not miss curfew. Nice young girls did not smoke. Nice young girls did not drink. Nice young girls did not talk back to their mothers. Nice young girls went to college. Nice young girls made their mothers proud.

Penelope had memorized those rules and at least twenty more. Most importantly, she had obeyed them.

Humph! Thelma thought she had it so hard, that her life was too sheltered. She should have grown up in the House of Webster, then she'd have something to complain about.

When the friendship between Crenshaw and Thelma first started, it had seemed like it was going to be one of those high school, study buddy type of things that end as quickly as they begin. Penelope hadn't given the relationship much thought. Crenshaw was a client, and if Thelma was nice to him, it would be good for business. But this . . . this was a romance and Penelope was afraid. It was so easy for a nice young girl to get into a mess that sometimes took years to fix. Some messes couldn't ever be fixed. No matter what happened, Crenshaw's parents were rich. And his father was famous. Money and celebrity could do a whole lot of fixing, no matter how big the mess. But what if the boy was in the habit of carrying drugs? What if they were found in his car during a routine traffic stop? What if Thelma was in the car with Crenshaw? What would happen to Thelma?

She'll take the weight, that's what, Penelope thought grimly. No matter what happened, the cashless, unknown girl would be branded a hussy, a floozy, a trickster girl who had gotten Bustacap's boy into trouble.

I've sacrificed too much for that girl! Penelope thought angrily. *He was probably about to touch her breast or something and then they heard me coming down the stairs. And she was probably about to let him! Right here in my house!*

She bounded down the steps and rushed full steam into the living room.

Crenshaw was sitting on the floor, drinking from a can of orange soda and laughing at something Chris Rock was saying on TV.

Thelma was on the other side of the room, watching the same TV show while fixing the hem on her black skirt.

Penelope felt like a fool. She ran back up the stairs without saying a word to either of them.

Chapter II

THELMA

Thelma could not understand how Penelope could be so stupid. Every time Crenshaw spent an evening in their home, her mother did the same thing. Listen for silence and then creep down the stairs. Didn't she think they were hip to the game by now and had found a way to get around her tactics?

What they usually did was make out in the kitchen. Thelma rattled the dishes in the rack with one hand while caressing Crenshaw's face with the other. Crenshaw, meanwhile, held her tightly around the waist. When they finished kissing, they scampered back to the living room.

Didn't Penelope think it odd that every time she came downstairs, they were on opposite sides of the room? Didn't she wonder why the two of them never sat side by side on the sofa?

This time, Thelma groaned aloud when Penelope fled back upstairs. "How can a mental health professional be so fucked-up?"

"Don't knock it," Crenshaw said. "If my parents weren't paying her so much money, I wouldn't be allowed over here at all."

"True. She probably wouldn't even let me talk to you."

They laughed heartily.

"I can't wait until I turn eighteen," Thelma groused.

"That's a whole year and a half away," he replied. "So let's not even talk about that."

Thelma shrugged. She wasn't worrying about anything. If Penelope tried to end her relationship, they would just take off in Crenshaw's car.

"I'm gonna have to call Mama to pick me up."

The battery in Crenshaw's car had died just as he pulled up in front of her house two hours before.

"Maybe you'd better call her now before it gets too late. If she has to get out of bed, she's gonna really get ticked off."

Crenshaw snorted. "She's not going to bed until all my dad's videos run out and she has two six-packs of beer under her belt."

Thelma didn't say anything. If she agreed that Shareeka was too obsessed with his dad's past, he might tell his mother and hurt her friendship with the older woman. If she said that Crenshaw needed to cut his mother some slack, then he would start ranting and raving about how fucked-up his father was.

She couldn't win.

"Yeah," he said. "I better call her."

He pulled out his cell phone and Thelma listened as he barked instructions to Cheery. Finally, he hung up.

"Why didn't you talk directly to your mother? Suppose Cheery falls asleep without telling her."

"She won't. Besides, now I only have to hear Mama bitch about the whole thing one time. If she came to the phone, she would have bitched now and then bitched again when she got here."

"Why? You didn't kill the battery."

Crenshaw sighed. "It doesn't matter."

They dropped the subject and watched television until Shareeka's car horn blared from outside.

The two lovers kissed a passionate good-bye and then Thelma trudged up to bed, wishing that Crenshaw was able to come with her.

Chapter 12

SHAREEKA

The car sailed smoothly through the quiet streets of Hercsville while Shareeka ran her mouth a mile a minute.

"My son is goin' with this real nice girl. Her name is Thelma. She and me . . . we really good friends . . . we are so close . . . I hope me and Cheery get to be close like that. Thelma is like my own daughter."

"That's nice," Asha replied.

"Yeah. I used to wonder what thangs was gonna be like when Crenshaw started dating."

"Your son's name is Crenshaw?"

"Yeah," Shareeka said proudly. "We're from California."

"I'm from New York but my name isn't Harlem." Asha laughed.

Shareeka laughed too and glanced at her appraisingly. "Do you always say what's on your mind?"

"No," Asha replied. "If I did that, nobody would be speaking to me right now."

"Nobody like who?"

"Like my mother-in-law for one."

"I love my mother-in-law," Shareeka said wistfully. "I miss her."

"Did she pass away?"

"No. She's in L.A. with the rest of my family and my husband's family. That's where my ass belongs too, but my husband ain't tryin' to hear it."

"Why? Is he from here?"

"Hell no!"

"Oh."

"We're here because of some business stuff."

She started to tell Asha how badly she missed the West Coast but decided that it wasn't a good idea to put her business out in the street. After all, she and Asha had just met.

"Thelma's mother is a trip, girl."

"What do you mean?"

"She's a snotty, stuck-up, bourgie bitch. I can't stand the way she treats Crenshaw, but I keep my mouth shut for him and Thelma's sake. Anyway, we got to deal with her because my son's teachers say that he needs therapy and she is the only shrink in Hercsville. You got kids?"

"Not yet."

"What you waitin' on?"

"I just got married a year ago. Maybe we'll start a family after I get our house in shape."

"So how you like Hercsville?"

"We just got here so I don't know. You're the first person I met."

"Gurl . . . these bitches out here got their ass on their shoulder. I only made one friend so far and I been here almost three years. Her name is Nancy. She's an actress. A lot of folks out here are in show business."

"Nancy got kids?"

Shareeka giggled. "Naw. What she got is a trifling-ass man that she supports and dreams. Stupid-ass dreams about marrying Denzel Washington."

"Denzel? Do y'all know Denzel?"

"I met him once when we still lived in California. Nancy wants to get with him. Seriously."

"He's married."

"Gurl . . . you gotta meet Nancy. She's a real kindhearted sister.

Smart as hell, but she lives in her own world when it comes to Denzel. It's some real crazy shit like she says that his lips give her confidence before she goes onstage. She got a lot of pictures of him and shit. Like I said, it's real crazy. But all show people are crazy."

Chapter 13

NANCY

Lying in her four-poster bed, covered by a pink satin comforter, Nancy recalled the sinister-sounding woman who had called almost four weeks before. *If you can figure out my identify and the reason why I hate you, I'll let you live also. If you can't, I will kill you and Bruce.*

Crazy bitch.

Nancy also thought about what Mama had said about the situation. "Don't change your number. She could be a nut. But if she ain't, you need to know what's goin' on in her head."

What Mama and the crazy woman didn't know was that she didn't have much money. There were the monthly mortgage payments, utility bills, car note on her Benz, fees for the publicity firm that kept her name in the news, and a personal trainer. There were weekly payments to her hairdresser, manicurist, gardener, housekeeper, agent, voice coach, drama coach, dance instructor, accountant, and administrative assistant. She also purchased at least ten romance novels per week and as much Denzel Washington memorabilia as she could get her hands on. Any money left over went for food or Bruce's airfare. He flew from comedy club to comedy club, trying to get the big break that would lead him to every comedian's dream, an appearance on *The David Letterman Show*.

The woman has probably jumped her crazy ass off a bridge, Nancy thought. Still, something in her gut was warning her to be careful. It was eleven o'clock. She decided to go downstairs and call Gail Strachan, her assistant. She stood in her floor-length, satin nightgown and dialed from the kitchen phone.

Gail screamed a hello. The music in her house was deafening.

"Gail, it's Nancy. Could you turn the music down for a moment, please?"

She waited until there was quiet.

"Gail, have you been getting any strange phone calls at the office?"

"What do you mean?" Gail was a tall, big-boned woman but her normal speaking voice sounded like Minnie Mouse's.

Nancy coughed. "Threatening calls, maybe? Or someone asking questions about my family?"

"No. Is something wrong?"

"I got an odd call."

"When?"

"A few weeks ago. I meant to ask you about it then, but things have been so crazy what with the holidays and all. . . ."

"No, everything is fine at the office. I do have a stack of checks that I need you to sign. Can you stop by tomorrow?"

"Sure. Sorry to bother you at home."

"No problem."

Nancy was wide-awake and feeling anxious. Bruce was out of town again. She had not mentioned the phone calls to him. Bruce was a laid-back sort of man, not prone to over-the-top scenes of jealousy, but he detested secrets. When he felt she was hiding something, he became cold and sarcastic. She didn't feel like dealing with it.

Nancy settled into an armchair and tried to concentrate on a romance novel. There was a rustling sound outside the window. She wanted to get up, push the drapes aside, and look outside but she didn't dare. She put the book down and listened closely. A twig snapped. There was a pitter-patter sound. A running sound. But the pitter-patter was too light for adult footsteps. Maybe if a six-month-old baby could run, it would sound like that.

Nancy's mouth felt dry. Her hands were shaking. She needed a drink. Maybe her friend, Shareeka, felt like going for a ride.

Shareeka answered her cell phone on the first ring and Nancy sent silent thanks up to God.

"Hello?"

"Shareeka, can you come get me?"

"Come get you? From where?"

"My house."

"Gurl, I got a strange woman in my car and I gotta get her home. Can I call you back?"

Nancy suddenly felt desperate. "Please come now."

"Gurl, I'm not in the mood for no games. What's the matter with you?"

"Shareeka, I'm not playing a joke."

"What is going on?"

"I'll explain later."

Nancy could picture Shareeka, decked out in some brassy, gold outfit with her hair gelled to within an inch of its life and tied up in a do-rag.

"Why are you whispering, Nancy? Is this about that sucker-ass Bruce?"

"Stop it. This isn't about a man. Someone is threatening to kill me. Plus, there is a noise in my yard. Like somebody is running."

"Say what?"

"I'm serious."

"Tell me what happened."

Nancy gave her a detailed rundown of the two calls and the pitter-patter sounds outside.

"Did you call the police?"

"No."

"Call the police right now. I'm coming over."

Nancy hung up and dialed 911.

While she waited for the police and Shareeka to arrive, Nancy called the hotel in Los Angeles where Bruce was staying. Not to tell him anything. Just to hear his voice and know that at least one part of her life was functioning normally. It was six in the evening on the West Coast, but Bruce's voice sounded muffled and groggy when he answered the phone.

"Hey, baby. Are you all right?"

"I'm fine. I just wanted to hear your voice, that's all."

"Wow. That's real nice."

Nancy smiled. It wasn't like her to call when he was out of town, and Bruce didn't know how to react.

"How did your meetings go today?"

He sighed. "Not good, baby."

"I'm sorry."

"Me too."

"Maybe tomorrow will be better."

His voice changed from glum to upbeat. "You're right. I must remain optimistic."

"When are you coming home?"

"Sunday night. Did you forget?"

Tonight was only Friday.

They made kissy sounds at each other before hanging up.

She paced the apartment, wringing her hands. When the bell rang, the sound startled her.

Two cops stood awkwardly in the foyer until she invited them into the living room, where they perched on the edge of the sofa and opened their notebooks. One of them, Officer Newburgh, was short with salt-and-pepper hair. The other, Officer Ryan, was tall and had the open, baby face of a rookie.

"Why don't you start at the beginning?"

She began with the first phone call and ended with the pitter-patter sounds and her frantic plea to Shareeka.

The older cop scratched his ear. "And you recognized the voice both times?"

"Yes, but I don't have any idea who would do something like this."

"Do you have any enemies, Miss St. Bart?"

She squirmed in the armchair. "Not anymore. There was a woman who hated me about two years ago, but we straightened everything out, and anyway, this isn't her style. She always identi-fied herself when she called and just said what she had to say."

The rookie spoke up. "Maybe we should pay her a visit?"

Nancy held up a hand to stop them. "I'd rather you didn't. It was a pretty nasty business, and there is no point in stirring it all up again, because it was definitely not her voice on the phone."

They both shrugged impatiently.

"In that case, there is nothing we can do," Newburgh said.

The two men left.

Shareeka Ellison pulled up as the two men were leaving. Crenshaw was with her and some lady that Nancy had never seen before. She didn't like letting strangers in, but there was no way to ask her to stand outside without being rude.

Nancy and Shareeka embraced and then Shareeka peered around anxiously as if Nancy's would-be killer was hiding in a closet.

"What on earth is going on?" she asked. "I saw two cops leaving. What did they say?"

"The cops wrote everything down and asked if I had any enemies. The only person I could think of was Ivie."

"Ivie?"

"Vernon's wife."

"Have you heard from him?" Shareeka asked sharply.

"No. I told them it's been two years. They wanted to contact Ivie anyway, but I nixed that idea."

"You still haven't told me everything that your caller said."

Nancy ran it down.

"It probably was Ivie," Shareeka mused.

"Why would she threaten me after all this time?"

"Maybe Vernon is staying out all night again and she thinks you're back on the scene."

"I doubt that Vernon will ever cheat on her again."

Shareeka snorted. "He's probably had ten mistresses since the two of you stopped seeing each other."

That remark stung but it also made Nancy feel better. She gave Crenshaw a hello kiss. Shareeka introduced her to Asha, and Nancy's eyes stopped darting about and her breathing returned to normal.

Suddenly it was an ordinary Friday evening and she felt foolish about dragging a busy mom like Shareeka out of her home for no good reason.

Shareeka started to laugh. "Poor stupid Ivie. Vernon is fucking around again and this time she decided to scare your ass."

Her booming laughter was infectious and soon all three women were chuckling too.

"Come on in," Nancy said.

Chapter 14

ASHA

I recognized Nancy Rosa St. Bart as soon as she opened the door. She plays a hairdresser named Glory Newton on this soap opera called *The Bridesmaid*. It comes on right before *The Price Is Right* and I watch it once in a while. The show is set in a small unnamed midwestern town and got its name because the richest woman in town who rules everybody was once a bridesmaid to the second most powerful woman in town. Their fractured friendship and mutual loathing are the basis of all the town's drama. Glory does everyone's hair, tries to help everyone solve their problems, and is sort of like the town mama. I've always been starstruck, so when she opened the door for me and Shareeka, I had to stop myself from behaving like some teenaged fan at a rap concert.

When we stepped inside, I almost went into shock. Starting with the foyer, which was where we were standing, every inch of wall space was covered with images of Denzel Washington. *Surely, they can't be in every room,* I thought. So I explained to Nancy that I was new to Hercsville and asked if she would mind showing me around. She was very gracious as we went on a mini-tour of her living space. There was not one wall in any of the four bedrooms, the kitchen, the den, the dining room, the office, the library that did not have pictures of Denzel Washington on them from floor to ceiling. There were color photos, black-and-whites, newsprint, magazine cutouts, movie posters, life-sized cardboard images. It was scary as hell.

When we got back to Shareeka and Crenshaw, who were waiting in the living room, I cleared my throat and summoned the courage to ask, "Are you going to film something here about Denzel?"

She laughed and the sound was much lighter than it was on television. As Glory, she sounded like a middle-aged woman. In person, it sounded like the laughter of a young girl. "No, honey. I just keep a few pictures around for inspiration. Show business is tough and life is worse. So when I need a pick-me-up, I just look at Denzel's lips and everything is fine again."

Shareeka nodded happily. "Everybody got their own thing to keep 'em goin'."

Crenshaw and I exchanged glances, and his face showed what was running through my mind. *Something is real wrong with this picture.*

Nancy said, "Sit down. Anybody want coffee?"

"Gurl, I left Cheery home all by herself. I got to get back."

"Why didn't you bring her with you?"

Shareeka explained all the incidents that had led us up to this point.

"Welcome to Hercsville," Nancy said to me. "What street do you live on?"

"Concourse Street."

"What do you do?"

My brain started churning. Maybe this crazy bitch could get me a job in television. "I'm just a production assistant for a couple of cable TV shows, music videos, stuff like that, but my husband's family owns a chain of restaurants. That's why we can afford to live here."

"Which restaurants?"

"Dang, girl. Why you interviewing this poor child?"

"I don't mind. It's the Seabrook Soul Food chain."

Nancy seemed to relax. "Good. I don't mean to be nosy, but

some crazy stuff has been happening in my life lately. I don't know for a fact who exactly is behind it, so I'm just being careful."

Shareeka moved toward the door. "Don't worry. Come spend the night at my house. Dayshawn has enough guns up in there to blow the shit out of any maniac who shows his face."

"I'm hungry," Crenshaw announced.

"You shoulda ate at your woman's house," Shareeka replied. "What's the matter? Thelma's stuck-up mama wouldn't feed you?"

Crenshaw didn't answer.

By this time we were all crowding into Shareeka's car.

"What you want, baby?" Nancy asked Crenshaw. "I'll buy it for you."

He shrugged and looked out the window.

Shareeka backed out of the driveway. "Crenshaw, I was eating fried shrimp before I had to come get yo ass. There's a lot more waiting to be cooked in the refrigerator. We can just throw them in some grease and they'll be done in a minute. You want me to make some french fries, too?"

He nodded.

I wondered what Shareeka and her husband did for a living and if their house was as big as mine and Nancy's. She seemed awfully ghetto for Hercsville.

"I could go for some shrimp, too," Nancy said.

Shareeka turned around and looked at me, slumped in the backseat. "Do you want to join the party, Asha?"

Actually, I wanted to get in my car and go home. But I was in the presence of a celebrity, had made up a lie connecting me to show business, and I had to keep playing my hand until I landed a job on the soap opera. That would show Nick's ass that I could find something to do.

"Sure." I grinned.

Shareeka and Nancy talked about the strange phone calls until we reached what appeared to be a gated community on Woodycrest Drive. Shareeka pulled out a gadget, pressed a button, and the gate opened.

"What is the name of this development?" I asked.

Both women laughed.

"It's called Shareeka's house," Nancy answered.

My eyes bulged out of their sockets as the car made its way up the longest tree-lined driveway that I'd ever seen. Finally we came to a stop in front of a columned mansion that was easily twenty-five thousand square feet in size, resting on about fifty acres of land.

By this time, my hand was pressed against my mouth in shock. When I realized what I was doing, I took my hand away and adopted a blasé seen-it-all attitude. If there was one thing I knew about rich people, it was that they don't like to be seen as different. Ain't that some dumb shit?

Whatever.

It wouldn't take me long to figure out what the deal was with Miss Shareeka. It would take longer for me to figure out how to get closer to her and learn how to get a spread like this for myself. As we walked into her gilt-mirrored hallway, I wished that Nick was beside me to see how Asha Mitchell Seabrook was supposed to be living. This place made my new house look like a cracker-jack box, and my interest in decorating it went right out the window.

Shareeka looked at me apologetically. "I'm just too tired to do the tour tonight, honey. That's okay, right?"

Nancy said, "I know I'm not walking up and down with y'all."

"It's beautiful," I breathed. I couldn't help myself. "How many rooms do you have?"

Shareeka stopped and thought about it. "A lot."

Crenshaw gave me the details. "We have a movie theater, a bowling alley, an indoor pool, a gym, a guest house, a music studio, and five bedrooms. Now, can we please fry the shrimp?"

Nancy pulled his sleeve playfully. "You forgot the five bathrooms, two offices, three living rooms, the den, the conference room, the media room, and that gigantic tennis court out back."

I followed the three of them a few feet, where we turned into a mirrored room that held the longest and only circular pink sofa that I had ever seen. The walls were done in pink suede. There was a glass coffee table, silver lamps, and a big-screen TV with surround sound. A pile of DVDs were on the table.

"Oh no," Nancy groaned.

"Not Dad's videos, again," Crenshaw chimed in.

Nancy turned to me. "Her husband used to be a big-time singer and she watches the videos, the interviews, home movies . . . a whole bunch of his shit over and over till it can make you want to puke."

Shareeka placed her hands on her hips, pretending to be angry. "There are a lot of TV sets in this house. Nobody has to watch this with me."

"Let's go and make some food," Crenshaw said to Nancy.

They were gone in a millisecond.

"Later for them," Shareeka said. "Do you like rap music, Asha?"

"Some of it," I answered truthfully.

"What about The Gangbangers?"

She looked over my shoulder and smiled. I felt a presence behind me, but before I could turn around, a baritone rang out. "Don't nobody wanna see that shit."

I pivoted on one foot and found myself face-to-face with Bustacap, one of the most famous rappers in history and the object of many of my fantasies back in my junior high school days.

It was love at first sight.

Chapter 15

SAUNDRA

We wrote out the checks and came up two hundred dollars short. Some bill was not going to get paid. Yero and I were curled up around each other on the living room floor.

"We need to borrow some money. Like five thousand dollars to get us caught up."

Yero said nothing so I took a deep breath and rushed on. "Asha wouldn't mind."

He sat upright and glared down at me. "That is the worst idea you ever had. Y'all are just going to start arguing and you'll be upset for weeks. Besides, how will that make me look?"

"It'll make you look like a smart man who knows when to make a necessary move."

"Why do you want to borrow money from Asha of all people?"

That might sound like a stupid question, but me and Asha have argued about money ever since we became women. She is a materialistic, moneygrubbing, gold-digging person. It used to make me angry, but now that she has married I don't worry about her pissing off the wrong man and getting herself killed. The problem is that she always used to say that one day I'd realize that life is all about money and then ditch my holistic lifestyle. Yero and I don't want her to say I Told You So.

"Well, the smart thing to do would be to find a cheaper apartment, but every apartment in New York is expensive these days, so we don't have that option. If I could get a better-paying job, I would. But I'm lucky to have the job I do. I don't have any skills, Yero. Besides drawing and sewing, I'm not trained to do anything."

He stroked his chin. "Why do we have to stay in New York?"

"What do you mean?"

"I mean, there is no law that says just because we were both born here, we have to stay here. We're free adults. Let's just move to a cheaper city."

"Yero?"

"What?"

"What about your job?"

"I'm a federal employee. The post office will transfer me out of New York City if I want to go."

"I don't want to leave my family."

He laughed. It wasn't a pleasant sound. "I'm your family."

I hugged him. "You know what I mean."

The phone rang and I ran to answer it. It was Asha. She was looking for her husband.

"He left about fifteen minutes ago, Asha. By the time the three of us went through all the wine, I figured he was too drunk to stumble out of here. You know, the yellow cabs don't come up to Harlem at night. He would have had to take a Gypsy cab and they would have charged him forty dollars or more."

"Okay. Listen . . . I've got a story to tell you that's going to knock your socks off."

"Asha, why are you just now checking up on Nick? It's almost noon. Weren't you worried a long time ago?"

"I didn't get home until six in the morning, drunk as hell. I just woke up."

"You went dancing by yourself?"

"Saundra, please shut the fuck up. I want to tell you about my evening."

I was quiet as she told me about the car crash and the strange woman with the Denzel fixation who was getting threatening calls.

"I'm glad you're all right, sweetie. That could have been a nasty accident."

"But wait—"

"Shareeka sounds all right, but I think you should stay away from Nancy whatever her name is. She sounds like a real loony tune."

"Saundra, you'll never guess who Shareeka is married to."

"Who?"

"Guess."

"Asha, I have no idea."

"I'll give you a hint."

"Go ahead."

I rapped:

> *Recognize*
> *Snap those thighs*
> *You could roll in my ride*
> *Last honey lied*
> *I'm untied*
> *Recognize*
> *Snap those thighs*

"Oh, my God!" she squealed. "One of The Gangbangers?"

"Listen, Saundra."

I picked up my story outside nutty Nancy's house and took it through the gate and up to the mansion. She was practically hyperventilating as I told her about the magnificent hallway and Shareeka's promise to give me a tour. Then, when she could take it no longer, I laid it on her. "Girlfriend is married to Bustacap!"

"*Whaaat?*"

"You heard me."

"Oh, shit, Asha!"

"Saundra, you remember all that trash Nick was talking about how I'm acting like a fifties housewife and I need to find something to do?"

"Yeah," she said cautiously.

"I just found it."

"Asha, what are you up to?"

"Every year *Vanity Fair* magazine publishes a music issue and they talk about the moguls and stuff in the recording industry. Well, last year they featured Dayshawn Ellison. Apparently, he hates to be reminded of his gangsta rapping days and will snap your head off if you call him Bustacap. Anyway, according to *Vanity Fair*, between his record company, film production business, some kind of licensing stuff, and his acting career, the muthafucka is now worth three hundred million dollars."

Saundra whistled.

"I told Nancy and Shareeka that I'm a production assistant who works on film and video."

I had to laugh at that. It was so Asha. My sister thinks fast on her feet and doesn't hesitate to jump off a diving board without knowing how to swim. "How do you plan to get your hands on Bustacap's dollars and cents?"

There was silence on the end of the line.

"Asha?"

"I'm not going to answer that because I don't want to get into an argument with you."

"I'm too tired to argue, Asha. Just don't do anything stupid."

"Yeah. Enough about me. What's up with you and Yero? Y'all both look sad."

"Everything's all right."

"Bullshit."

I couldn't say anything because Yero was lying right behind me. "I'll talk to you later, okay?"

"Saundra."

"What?"

"It was love at first sight."

"Who?"

She laughed softly. "Me and Bustacap, of course."

Then Asha hung up the phone.

That was it. There was no way I was leaving New York now. Somebody had to be the voice of reason in Asha's life, and that job had always been mine.

Chapter 16

PENELOPE

Tremont Avenue, which sat directly in front of Woodycrest Drive where the hip-hop and soap opera stars lived, was said to be the classiest place in Hercsville.

Reverend Herbert Best, Janice Webster, Mayor Nelson Brown, and the Brewsters all lived on Tremont. So did the bank president, two doctors, a couple of lawyers, and a sprinkling of corporate executives who worked in Manhattan.

They all saw themselves way above the super-rich but gaudy entertainers of Woodycrest Drive, sneered at the middle managers, restaurateurs, and others who inhabited Concourse Street, and didn't even speak to the maids, chauffeurs, maintenance men, and so forth who lived across town in Flash Place.

On the last night of every month, Janice, Nelson, Penelope, and Herbert all gathered at one of their houses for what they called the town council meeting, but since there was rarely any official business to discuss, it usually degenerated into a gossip-fest. Tonight they gathered at the mayor's kitchen table.

"Nice spread," observed Penelope, who couldn't wait to dive into the roast beef, baked chicken, potato salad, chocolate chip cookies, and pitcher of iced tea.

"Sure is," Reverend Best said. "I feel like royalty."

Nelson chuckled. "Go ahead! Enjoy!"

"Yes, let's eat. I've got a really exciting idea tonight and I can't wait for y'all to hear it," Janice said.

"Sounds like I'm going to need something stronger than iced tea," joked the Reverend, who secretly detested Janice.

Janice ignored the remark as she fixed herself a plate. There had been many times when she wanted to cuss out Herbert Best, but even though she wasn't a devoutly religious person, it didn't seem like a good idea to aim such vile language at a man of the cloth.

They made small talk while they ate, and it wasn't until after Mayor Nelson Brown's maid had cleared the table that the meeting actually started.

"The teenagers of Hercsville have made an unusual request," he said. "They want to change a few of the town's street signs. I don't see anything wrong with it."

"Why?" the reverend asked.

Penelope shrugged. "Which teenagers?"

Janice waved a hand dismissively. "Just tell them to forget it."

Nelson cleared his throat. "Okay. Next order of business?"

"Janice, why don't you just tell us what to talk about?" the Reverend said.

She ignored the sarcasm. "Well, since you asked, I've been thinking that this town needs to expand. With just a little work, we could create a few more streets behind Concourse and do the same thing behind Woodycrest. It would be a great new source of revenue for Hercsville and create more jobs for the poor people on Flash Place."

"That's not a bad idea," the Reverend admitted.

Penelope hated it. "Do you know how many trees would have to die in order to build all those new houses? We'd have to cut down half the woods behind both streets. It's awful."

"Dr. Penny," Nelson said quietly, "there are a lot of trees on Long Island. The world won't come to an end if we have to cut down about twenty of them."

"Besides," Penelope continued, "we should be trying to close Woodycrest down instead of moving new people in there."

"Penny, we all know that the rappers are gaudy, vulgar people, but right now they have more money than anyone else in Hercsville and they don't mind spending it," Janice reminded her. "All we have to do is make sure that no more of those young hip-hoppers get in. The soap opera people are quiet and they do keep to themselves."

"Oh, come on, Mama!" Penelope screeched. "The whole point of moving to a town like Hercsville is for peace, privacy, and a zero crime rate. What do you think is going to happen if we keep expanding?"

"Calm down," Nelson laughed. "I seriously doubt that a group of television actors are going to move here and become serial killers."

"We aren't going to get any more TV people. Just a new batch of dirty rappers."

Nelson ignored her. "Okay, Janice. I'll take it up with the authorities, contractors, governor, city hall, and everyone else. This is going to take a lot of paperwork and a whole lotta man-hours. Plus, I'm going to have to grease a few government palms."

"We have to spend money to make money," Janice observed.

Reverend Best chimed in. "Let's hold a fund-raiser."

The mayor agreed. "Great idea but let's think a little harder. Suppose we form a committee of four Hercsville citizens to help us with the whole expansion project. If we call for volunteers, then folks won't feel like we're shoving this thing down their throats."

Janice beamed. "We'll have to make sure that every part of this town is represented. Shareeka Ellison can represent the hip-hoppers. She'll be easy to handle and, besides, she doesn't care a whit about Hercsville. From what I hear, she misses her native California and can't wait to leave the East Coast behind."

The Reverend wrote Shareeka's name down on a pad. "Who else?"

Penelope sighed. "Well, Nicholas Seabrook's new wife doesn't work either. I've never met the woman, but the Seabrooks are a respectable clan. I'm sure the bride is educated and dignified."

There were nods around the table and Asha Mitchell Seabrook's name was added to the list.

Janice frowned. "We don't have any men."

"What about Grant Pearson?" the mayor asked.

Penelope shook her head. "He's a movie actor. We need people with semiregular schedules."

The mayor replied, "Who cares if he doesn't show up at the meetings? His name will help us raise money."

The Reverend waited for the silence that indicated approval and then wrote Grant's name with a flourish.

"I say we ask Theresa Tanner to head the committee."

Mayor Nelson Brown was in such a state of denial that he actually believed no one knew he was in love with the actress.

"You're a moron," Penelope said. "I can't believe that you'd put the whole town at risk just to spend more time with that hot-in-the-pants little Jezebel."

Nelson rose from his seat and raised a hand.

Before he could say anything, Janice interceded by pulling him back down. "Penny, that was truly unnecessary. You really need to apologize to the mayor."

Janice said all that while fixing her daughter with a stare that could have punctured granite.

"Sorry."

Nelson adjusted his shirt. "Just for the record, I am not romantically or sexually involved with Theresa Tanner."

Everyone in the room knew that he wanted to be.

Reverend Best neatly sidestepped the issue. "So it is decided. Our mayor will approach the proper authorities and get us a yes or no on the proposed expansion of Hercsville."

"I hope they say no," Penelope moaned. "We need to concentrate on getting people like the Ellisons out of Hercsville, not how to move some more of them in."

The mayor saw his opportunity and struck back. "Oh, so that's your problem. You're worried about little hot-in-the-pants Thelma fraternizing with little Crenshaw Ellison."

Penelope reached across the table and slapped the shit out of him.

Janice and the Reverend watched the attack in total disbelief.

The mayor rubbed his injured cheek. "I deserved that. Reverend

Best, we've heard from everyone else tonight. Do you have a topic you wish to discuss?"

The reverend actually had wanted to talk about raising money for the poverty-stricken children of Flash Place, but the slap had done him in. He shook his head in the negative.

"Then this meeting is over. You can see yourselves out."

With that, Mayor Nelson Brown glared at Penelope, got up, and stalked out of his own dining room.

Chapter 17

THELMA

Crenshaw and Thelma loved to smoke weed. They smoked it in his Lexus and whenever they were laid up like tonight in bed together in his father's suite at Manhattan's Parker Meridien Hotel.

"How late can you stay out?" he asked.

Thelma stretched and yawned, snuggling farther down into his arms. "I dunno . . . about midnight, I guess."

He sucked his teeth. "That's still daylight."

"Well, I'm sorry that my mother is not down like your parents."

"I'm ready to party."

"Puh-leeze, Crenshaw." Thelma pulled the covers over their naked bodies. "I'm a better dancer than you and I can hold my liquor better, too. So don't go trying to make me feel bad because I can't hang out."

He grinned and played with her hair. "Let's just do what we want. Just this one time."

They ended up at a rowdy spot in Brooklyn called The Hut. The place was rocking a female deejay and a hellified sound sytem. There were at least two hundred young people, packed in the gigantic room. Even though it was cold outside, The Hut's interior was way too hot. Crenshaw pulled Thelma onto the dance floor and they were soon huffing, puffing, jumping up and down, drenched in sweat.

By 3:00 a.m. they were drunk. Thelma's feet were hurting and their stomachs were growling.

Crenshaw held Thelma tightly and they moved . . . grinding to a slow jam.

"Call your mama and tell her that we're spending the night in Manhattan and then we'll go back to the Parker and chill."

"You're crazy," Thelma giggled.

But his request reminded her that she had not been in touch with Penelope all evening. She pulled her cell phone out, kissed Crenshaw on his thin lips, and went outside.

Penelope picked up on the first ring.

"Mama, it's me."

There was a huge sigh of relief on the other end. "Thank God you're all right."

"I'm sorry that I broke curfew, Mama."

"Where are you?"

"At a club in Brooklyn. I'm with Crenshaw."

Penelope practically spat the next words. "Get home. Now. And you're grounded for the next fucking month."

Thelma made her voice sound like that of a penitent eight-year-old. "I'm sorry, Mama. It won't happen again."

"You're right. It won't. Tell that little ragamuffin that if you're not home in an hour, I'm calling the police. Are we clear?"

"Yes."

Thelma rushed back into the club and broke the news to her totally stoned boyfriend.

"Damn, Thelma. Your moms just won't ease up."

"Not at all," Thelma agreed miserably.

Back in the car, Crenshaw pounded the steering wheel. "We got to think of something, Thelma. I can't go through this shit with your moms for another whole year."

"Crenshaw, just drive. We'll talk about it tomorrow."

"What else did she say?"

"She said I'm grounded."

"Shit!"

"My head hurts."

"Thelma, let's just tell her the truth."

"What is the truth?"

"That my pops keeps a suite at the Parker for business purposes and my parents know that I use it. Tell her that we're not always running around in clubs. Most of the time, we come to Manhattan and chill at the suite."

"Are you crazy? The first thing she'll figure is that we're having sex."

"We are. We use protection. So what?"

Thelma shook her head so hard, her earrings fell off. "Mama would probably ship me out of the country for good if I told her some shit like that. Now, keep your eyes on the road and get me home quick."

Crenshaw groaned. "If she calls the police on me, the reporters will be all over my father. He'll kill me."

The two young people headed back to Long Island wearing grim and angry faces.

Chapter 18

NANCY

Bruce had been away for two whole weeks this time, playing a series of gigs in Chicago. His plane was supposed to land at four o'clock and Nancy had planned a nice, romantic dinner for the two of them. By nine o'clock Bruce still wasn't home and the knot of anxiety in her stomach had turned to concrete.

At ten o'clock, she picked up the phone and dialed 911. The operator was in the middle of explaining that her dilemma was not technically an emergency when Nancy heard the sound of keys. She ran down the stairs and nearly knocked Bruce down when she flew into his arms. "Where have you been? I was scared to death!"

"Wow! Did a plane crash or something?"

Nancy kissed him passionately on the lips. "No. It's just that your plane got in five hours ago."

"I ended up changing my flight."

"Oh." The word sounded small and foolish.

Bruce removed the garment bag from his shoulder and peered intently at her drawn face. "Are you all right?"

Nancy forced a smile. "I've just been working too hard."

Bruce sighed wearily and headed for the stairs. "That makes two of us."

"Are you hungry? I can warm up the lasagna."

"No, but thanks."

"Well," she said, "let's both get some sleep."

He paused on the top step and turned around. "Not until you tell me why you're practically jumping out of your skin."

"It's a business thing. Don't worry. We can talk about it tomorrow."

He smiled. "Cool."

"Go to bed, sweetie. I'll be up in a minute."

The phone rang as Bruce climbed the steps.

"I'll get it!" Nancy yelled.

He gazed back down at her curiously.

She ran to the kitchen and picked up the wall phone. "Hello?"

The female voice sounded lazy. "So, bitch . . . what is my name?"

It was the moment Nancy had been waiting for. "I don't give a fuck."

There was a dry, mirthless chuckle. "That's the only honest thing you've ever said to me, Nancy."

The line went dead.

She started up the steps. Bruce was still standing there.

"Nancy," he said. "Cut the bullshit and tell me what is going on. You've been acting strange for weeks."

She took a deep breath. "I think you'd better sit down."

He ended up sitting on the bed.

Bruce never took his eyes off her as she paced back and forth while telling her story.

"Are you cheating on me again, Nancy?"

She sighed. "No, I'm not. What about you? Could this woman be connected to you in some way?"

Bruce's eyes widened. "Are you suggesting that I'm having an affair?"

"Come on, Bruce. Maybe some female likes you and is trying to bust us up."

"There is no one like that in my life."

A shadow crossed his face. Nancy saw that and a sudden flash of neediness in his eyes that she didn't understand.

When Bruce first came to live with her, she had studied his

every word and gesture, waiting for signs of propensity for abuse
or infidelity. Her previous lovers had all fallen into one of the two
categories. She was hoping for the last time that she had found
her Mr. Right—an honest, caring, ambitious, humble, faithful,
and hardworking black man. Actually, she was looking for a good
husband, but Bruce refused to get married until after he landed
a spot on *The Tonight Show*. The first time he told her that, she
started to throw him out. Then she decided that you had to respect a man for not trying to ride her coattails. He had never
asked her for an introduction to anyone on the soap opera or
mentioned the fact that he was a comedian when they went to social gatherings where soap opera people were in attendance.

Now, for the first time in their five-year relationship, something
wasn't right.

"Do you want to tell me something, Bruce?"

"Not about those phone calls. I swear, Nancy, they have nothing to do with me."

She stared at him hard and then smiled. "I believe you."

"We do need to talk, though. Just not tonight."

"About what?"

He patted the bed beside him. "In a few weeks, I'll tell you.
Now come sit down and give me a kiss."

Chapter 19

ASHA

The sugary sentiment of Valentine's Day had come and gone. The two dozen red roses had been sniffed and thrown away, the Godiva chocolates eaten, and life for the women of Hercsville had gone back to normal.

I was downstairs eating breakfast alone. Nick was still sleeping.

The telephone rang and I picked up the receiver with one hand and poured syrup on a stack of pancakes with the other.

"Hello?"

"Is this Asha Seabrook?"

Even though I had been married for a year, the name still sounded strange to my ears. "Uh . . . yes."

"Mrs. Seabrook, my name is Janice Webster and I'm editor in chief of the *Hercsville Democrat*. How are you?"

I sat down and took a bite of pancake. "We already get the paper."

"I'm not trying to sell you anything, dear. Hasn't your husband spoken to you about the Herscville Expansion Project?"

"My husband?"

"Yes . . . Nicholas Seabrook. We're creating a group of Hercsville citizens who will help our city council get the project under way and . . ."

I rolled my eyes. "I'm not a committee type of woman but thank you for calling."

"Oh, that's too bad. Grant Pearson will be so disappointed."

My heart nearly stopped. "Grant Pearson? You mean the actor?"

"Yes," Janice replied briskly. "He is on our committee but never mind, I'm sorry to disturb you."

I had been reading about Grant Pearson in the gossip columns for years. In his busy career as an actor, he had bedded just about every African-American actress on the East and West coasts, plus most of the white girls as well. He was tall, dark, handsome, had a wide chest and a smile that was sexy enough to melt frozen butter.

"Wait! Don't hang up!"

There was silence on the other end of the line.

"I mean . . . perhaps I could make time for the first meeting . . . you know . . . just to find out what it's all about."

"Wonderful." Janice couldn't keep a note of sarcasm from creeping into her voice. "Mr. Pearson will be in touch."

Nick walked in, still wearing his pajamas.

"Who was that?" he asked.

"Janice Webster. She's part of some committee that is working on expanding Hercsville."

He plopped himself into a chair. "Oh yeah. She cornered me in the supermarket a while back. Tried to get me to join up. I told her that I didn't have time but you might be interested."

"I told you and your mother that I'm not a committee person."

"Didn't sound that way a minute ago."

I sat down across from him. "Well, I figure that it won't hurt to check it out. Maybe I'll make some friends or something."

Nick squinted at me. "What are you up to?"

I feigned innocence. "Up to?"

"Yeah. Up to. I figured you'd turn her down."

"Then why'd you tell her to call me?"

He shrugged. "Just to get her off my own back."

"Well, now you can go tell your mother that I'm joining something. The two of you have been trying to turn me into a society type since we got married."

"That's what Seabrook women do."

"Good. So now you'll all be happy."

"I still say you're up to something."

I laughed and so did he.

"You may as well tell me what it is. I'm going to find out sooner or later."

I decided to toss him a bone. "Remember when I met those women . . . Shareeka and Nancy?"

He nodded.

"Well, I told them that I was a production assistant, which is almost true. That's going to be my new career."

"Production assistant? What is that?"

"Somebody who works on staff when a movie is getting filmed."

He said nothing.

"Anyway, there might be a show business person on this committee. I figure that if I'm nice and friendly, maybe it'll get me a job."

"Good," he replied. "You need to stay busy." He sniffed the air. "What did you have for breakfast?"

"Pancakes. You want some?"

"If it's not too much trouble."

I gave him a smile. "No, it's not too much trouble."

Our eyes met and, for just a minute, I caught a glimpse of the devil-may-care playboy that I used to know.

"Asha, can I talk to you about something?"

Uh-oh.

"Sure."

He paused for a moment to gather his thoughts. I busied myself around the kitchen making his breakfast.

"It's like this, Asha. Remember when I used to travel around the country checking up on the restaurant managers?"

"Nick, you just stopped doing that a few months ago. Of course I remember."

"Well, remember that I only took this new job working for Daddy in the New York office so that I could be home every night with you?"

I was getting irritated. "Get to the point, Nick."

"Well . . . it's like . . . I mean, I did the right thing. I figured that a married man should be home every night."

"And a married woman should act like a lady, have babies, and go to committee meetings," I replied.

He frowned. "Why you say it like that?"

"Because you never told me that you wanted me to change. You should have told me that before we got married."

We'd had this argument a dozen times.

"Asha, I don't want to get off the subject."

"What is the subject, Nick?"

He took a deep breath. "I hate working in the office pushing paper around. I miss being on the road. Now, I'm not saying that I'm going to make a change. It's just that I thought you should know why I'm so irritable a lot of the time. I just want to say that I'm sorry."

A few weeks ago, I would have told him in no uncertain terms that he was not going back on the road and leave me sitting in this big house for days at a time. But things were getting interesting in this new town. I had not heard any more from Nancy or Shareeka, but I had been thinking of just dropping by for a friendly hello. They were busy women, and if I wanted to get involved in their lives I'd have to jump-start the friendships. On top of that, this Webster woman was going to bring me face-to-face with Grant Pearson. Plus, I'd been researching the whole production assistant thing on the Internet. I sensed that a whole new world could open up for me if I played my cards right.

"Nick," I said sweetly, "if you don't like working in the company office, then don't work there. Tell your daddy that you want your old job back."

He waved a hand. "Aw, no, baby. I couldn't do that to you."

"I'm really serious about this movie work thing. Plus, I've been thinking about spending more time with Saundra. On top of all that, I've still got to decorate this big house. Do you, baby. Do you."

"It might cause problems between us," he protested.

"What will cause problems between us is a miserable-ass husband who hates his job."

He thought about that. "You've got a point there."

I poured batter into the frying pan. "Problem solved."

He watched me intently. "I don't have anything to worry about, do I, Asha?"

I stared him straight in the eye. "If you mean, will I commit adultery? it's a stupid question. A cheating woman will find a way even if her man works at home. Don't even start that shit."

"Forget I asked."

Of course I had thought about cheating when Shareeka's husband seemed to look me up and down with lust-filled eyes. Since then, I decided that the whole thing must have been my imagination. After all, if he'd really felt some heat, he would have looked me up. I'd also had some time to ask myself some serious questions. Would I have felt like I'd met my soul mate when he walked into the room if he had not been a famous man? If I had not spent so much time staring at posters and album covers with his face on them when I was a teenager? Did I really want to risk the only financial security I'd ever had by losing my husband? I'd had enough affairs with married men to know that they never leave their wives. Which means that if Bustacap and I did go to bed and Nick found out, I'd end up back in a tenement.

"No problem."

Nick, on the other hand, could cheat with anyone he liked and I'd still need him to maintain my new standard of living. I didn't like that. According to my Internet research, this production assistant thing could take me places if I worked hard and networked. I'm no stranger to hard work.

"So I'm going to talk to Dad on Monday. Okay?"

"Yes, sweetheart. It is okay."

He sighed and gave me a grateful smile. "I love you, Asha."

"I love you too, Nick."

It was true, I did love Nick. I just didn't like getting an ultimatum from him back when we were both seeing other people. But even back then, he was always my favorite companion and I looked forward to the days when he would breeze into town. He was full of life, sexually healthy, and always ready to crack a joke. Now he looked like every other businessman who rode into the city every day to crunch numbers before riding back to suburbia in the evening. He didn't have any jokes to tell me because there was nothing funny in the six-person office that he ran with his father.

Maybe if he went back on the road, the old Nick would return.

"So when are we going over to Bustacap's house?"

Nick had been beside himself with excitement when I told him about the brief meeting. Turned out he used to be a fan of The Gangbangers as well.

"I keep telling you that I never heard from Shareeka again."

"Well, call her up. Maybe she thinks that you don't want to be bothered. Especially since she hangs around with a crazy woman."

I placed a big plate of pancakes and bacon in front of him.

"She is crazy," I agreed. "That place looks like something out of a horror movie. I don't know what kind of man she lives with. I mean, who the hell would put up with that Denzel Washington fun house?"

"A man who has no place else to go."

I laughed. "You're probably right."

"So who is on this committee that you're joining? You said something about a show business connection."

"Grant Pearson."

He paused with his fork in midair. "You serious?"

"That's what she said."

"Damn. We must be the poorest people in this town."

That had never occurred to me, but now that the words had been uttered, I didn't like it. I had been on the bottom for a long time. It's not a pleasant place to be.

"Maybe not," I said cheerfully. "I'll check this town out thoroughly and let you know what's what."

He went back to eating. "Cool. So when you gonna call Shareeka? I really want to meet Bustacap. I want to ask him why The Gangbangers broke up."

"Nick, you've got to remember not to call him by that name. I read a long time ago that he fires anybody who slips up at work and calls him that. His name is Dayshawn Ellison."

"Dayshawn Ellison," Nick repeated. "So when you gonna call her?"

Chapter 20

SAUNDRA

Saundra sat on the edge of a chair in front of her supervisor's glass-topped desk. Josephina Helden read through the page of text that Saundra had written about the new trend in the design of ladies' purses. "Do you really like writing about fashion?"

"Don't you like it?"

Josephina smiled. "You are an adequate fashion writer. But just adequate."

Was she in danger of losing her job?

"I'll try harder. If you can just give me a hint as to what is wrong with the piece, I'll rework it tonight."

Josephina shoved the offending paper across her desk toward Saundra. "I don't think you have a passion for this type of work."

That was true.

"I've watched your eyes light up when the sample garments come in and you're touching the fabric. You're like a different person. That's where your passion is. Am I right?"

"Look, Josephina. I really enjoy working here at *Mode* magazine and I—"

Josephina held up a thin white hand. "Relax, Saundra. I'm not about to fire you."

Saundra's eyes were still wary. "Really?"

The elegant woman tossed her glossy brown hair and smiled.

"Really. I don't think you're cut out to be a fashion writer because you don't want to report on the product. You want to be a part of its creation. Am I right?"

"Well, I majored in fashion design but I couldn't find an entry-level job in the field. No one would give me a break."

"I understand, but don't throw your passion aside. Keep designing in your spare time, put together a portfolio, and knock on doors during your lunch hour. In the meantime, I'm going to give you something else to do here at *Mode*."

"What?"

"Saundra, don't look so scared. I'm not trying to trick you. Honest. It's just that I've been doing this for twenty years and I'm tired of traveling so much to fashion shows and studios. It occurred to me last night that you and I could create a new position. One where you're on the road when I don't feel like going or just can't make it. I haven't worked it all out in my head yet, but what do you think?"

"I think you're wonderful," Saundra gasped.

Josephina laughed as she looked at her naive assistant. "No, honey. I'm not all that. I've just bought a new country home, I have a new man, and this job isn't everything to me anymore. I can find a new editorial assistant in half an hour. But your dimples show when you see a spool of thread and you practically drool at the sight of an unfinished sketch. It would be crazy to waste that kind of enthusiasm."

Saundra smiled.

Josephina stood up. "In the meantime, just keep on doing the best you can. I'll come up with something."

Saundra stood above Yero, who was lying prone on the sofa, apparently exhausted from a hard day's work at the post office.

"Guess what?"

"I can't, honey. Just tell me."

"I got a promotion!"

Yero grinned and reached out for his wife. "See? You were going on and on about how you hated the job. How you were no good at it. And all the time, those folks knew they had a talented, stand-up sister on staff."

"Well, actually, I'm being promoted because my writing sucks."

"Huh?"

Saundra nudged his body aside so that she could sit next to him and caress his face. "They're giving me another position. One that'll get me from behind the desk and mixing with the fashion designers. I don't know if I'll get more money but . . ."

All of a sudden, Yero closed his eyes.

"Honey." Saundra patted his chest. "You okay?"

"I think I need to eat."

Saundra jumped up. "We're having veggie burgers and fries."

"That's fine."

Saundra put the meal together quickly.

They ate at the kitchen table.

"Yero, did you ever call that therapist?"

"Yes. I went to see her last week."

Saundra put her burger down. "What? Why didn't you tell me? What did she say?"

"I didn't tell you because there was nothing to tell. It's just like I told you. I don't need a shrink."

"Start at the beginning," Saundra demanded.

Yero sighed. "I called her up. Told her that I've been tired a lot and that my wife has diagnosed me with clinical depression. She said come on in. I did. We talked. She told me that the joint pain concerns her so I should go have a complete physical exam. I'm having one tomorrow. I already took the day off."

"You can have a physical problem like arthritis and still be clinically depressed," Saundra said stubbornly.

Yero continued as though she hadn't spoken. "She said that after the results from the physical, I should call her back and let her know what the deal is. Then we'll take it from there."

They continued eating in silence for a while and then Saundra said, "Do you want me to go with you tomorrow?"

Yero shook his head. "For what? If you want to come when I go for the results, that would make more sense."

He was right.

Yero reached for another french fry, then grabbed his stomach and grimaced with his eyes closed.

Saundra watched as beads of sweat appeared on his forehead. She pushed her chair back, rushed to the wall phone, and dialed 911.

"Saundra, I'm fine," he protested. Then he vomited up everything he had eaten and keeled over on the floor.

Chapter 21

PENELOPE

Dr. Penny hated it when a child's parent requested a meeting with her without divulging the nature of the get-together. Yet, Shareeka and Dayshawn Ellison had done just that and were on their way to her office.

They wouldn't have the nerve to object because Thelma was still on punishment and not allowed to socialize with Crenshaw. Would they? Surely they knew that no matter how much money she received from them, Thelma was still her child who had to abide by her wishes. Didn't they? Or did they wield so much power and influence in the entertainment world that the line between playacting and reality was beginning to blur?

Well, if they walked their expensively clad asses into her office throwing money around to get Thelma off punishment, she would give them an earful. That's what. A real earful.

She stood in front of the window, her arms crossed rigidly across her chest, and watched as a white stretch limousine pulled up and a chauffeur stepped out. He moved swiftly to the rear of the vehicle and opened the door with a flourish. Dayshawn stepped out and reached back in to help his wife.

The woman was wearing a wide fur hat and matching coat. Was it mink? She held her husband's hand and chattered as she stepped along in a beautiful pair of suede high-heeled boots.

She said something that cracked him up. He threw back his head and laughed loudly. The sound echoed in the cold winter air.

Penelope turned away from the window and opened the door of her office before they could knock.

She smiled broadly. "Mr. and Mrs. Ellison. I'm delighted to see you."

Shareeka grinned. "Hi, Dr. Penny. You're lookin' good."

Penelope smoothed her straight black skirt and checked her white silk blouse. It was spotless.

Dayshawn shook her hand pleasantly and they hung up their coats.

Penelope took her seat behind the desk and motioned them into two facing chairs.

"So what's new?"

"Dayshawn just got the green light to do a new movie," Shareeka beamed.

The family members revolved around the father as if he were the sun. Penelope felt a lump in her throat.

"Congratulations." She nodded at Dayshawn. "How is Cheery doing?"

They looked at each other as if they couldn't remember who Cheery was, and then Shareeka smiled pleasantly.

"My daughter is fine. In fact, she is the reason we stopped by."

Penelope was surprised. "Really?"

"Yes," Shareeka continued. "She's startin' to act up and stuff, so we figured she should start comin' here too. We want to know if we get a discount for havin' two kids here."

Penelope's first thought was that they should both be slapped. Hard. But she responded like a professional. "What do you mean by act up and stuff? What exactly has Cheery done?"

"She cussed out her teacher," Dayshawn laughed. "The way I see it, the man had it comin'. Cheery was caught chewing gum in class. All he had to do was make her throw it in the garbage. He told her to stand in the corner with chewing gum on her nose and she cussed his ass out. She did the right thing as far as I'm concerned. I don't think Cheery needs to see no shrink, but my wife dragged me here anyway."

"She didn't just curse Mr. Williamson out," Shareeka responded primly. "She threw a chair at him too. The principal says that she has anger issues and that they'll call Social Services if we don't get her some help."

Penelope wanted to say, *If you two self-centered assholes were my parents, I'd just hitchhike the fuck out of town,* but she didn't.

"By the way," Dayshawn asked casually, "how long is Thelma going to be on punishment for missing curfew? Crenshaw is mopin' around the house, don't know what to do with himself."

"Let's talk about Cheery. It sounds to me like she is just making a bid for attention."

"I spend time with my kids," Shareeka said.

Penelope looked her in the eye. "I don't mean spend time in the same room with her, Mrs. Ellison. I mean spend time with her talking about her or participating in an activity that she is interested in and that is designed for a child."

"What makes you think I don't do that?"

Penelope shrugged. "Intuition."

"Well, you're wrong."

"I've been wrong before. So tell me about your relationship with Cheery."

Shareeka counted on her fingers. "We watch videos together, we read stories, we talk."

"What kind of videos?"

Crenshaw had told Penelope about Shareeka's continuous viewing of The Gangbangers, so she now watched the woman's response very closely.

"Music videos."

"Really? Which groups does she like?"

"Well . . . uh . . . she uh . . . she likes a little rapper called Bow Wow."

"Wrong!" Dayshawn shouted. "Cheery don't even like rap music at all."

"She don't?" Shareeka was clearly astonished.

Dayshawn burst out laughing. "Hell no!"

"What made you think that she liked Bow Wow?" Penelope asked calmly.

"She has a poster of him in her room."

"Come on, Shareeka. You gave her the damn poster for her birthday. What was she supposed to do with it?"

Shareeka opened her mouth to respond, but Penelope held up a hand. "Stop." They both stared at her.

"I will start seeing Cheery once a week if that is what you and the school want, and no, you cannot have a discount. However, paying me will not solve the problem you have with Cheery. Nor will it solve Crenshaw's problems. What they both need is to be noticed and recognized as individual people. Not tiny accessories of a hip-hop star and his wife."

There, she'd said it. Inside, she was heated but outwardly she appeared calm, professional, and in control.

"How do we do that?" Dayshawn asked.

He looked genuinely puzzled while Shareeka just looked pissed off.

Penelope leaned forward. "Let's try an experiment. For the next thirty days, do not talk about yourselves or Dayshawn's professional activities in front of either child at all."

They looked lost.

"What should we talk about?" Dayshawn asked.

Shareeka still said nothing.

Penelope spoke gently to the man who truly seemed prepared to do whatever it took to help his kids. "If you're quiet, they'll talk about their own worlds and then you just respond. It'll be easier with Cheery because she is only ten years old. The boy is an adolescent. It is harder to get them to open up."

Dayshawn bristled. "Crenshaw ain't no boy. He's a man."

"No," Penelope said softly. "He is sixteen years old and he is a boy. If you handle him right, he'll become a wonderful man."

Shareeka sucked her teeth. "Puh-leeze. If The Gangbangers didn't become famous, out there on the streets of Los Angeles, he would have become a man in a hurry. His life would be different. This money done ruined everything."

Penelope saw what was coming.

"Ruined everything?" Dayshawn shouted. "Girl, you spend my money like it's going out of style. In fact, that's all you do is spend money and complain that we ain't still livin' in the fuckin' hood."

Shareeka stood up, enraged. "I do not complain about not livin' in no hood. I complain about yo ass walkin' around in those silly-ass suits tryin' to act like a white man. I complain about livin' in this cold-ass city. I want to go the fuck home."

He stood up too and faced her. "Then go! Planes leave New York every fuckin' hour. Go!"

Penelope raised her voice. "Have you two ever considered marriage counseling?"

They turned.

"I don't need no marriage counselor. I need Dayshawn to act like the man I married and I want all of us to go back to California."

Dayshawn grabbed his coat. "I'm outta here."

Shareeka ran after him without another word.

Penelope massaged her temples and sighed.

Chapter 22

ASHA

It was a Thursday afternoon and I was in the research room at the Donnell Library in Manhattan reading everything I could find on how movies and television shows were produced and what exactly a production assistant was supposed to do.

The news wasn't good.

From what I could tell, production assistants were whatever the director wanted them to be. Most of the time, the job meant that you were a combination of secretary, chauffeur, messenger, and errand runner. To make matters worse, the pay was lousy and the hours were ridiculous. Most of the time, a production was on call from sunup to sundown until the project was over. I had had visions of showing up in my cute designer outfits and learning how to write scripts and operate the cameras. It didn't work like that.

Worst of all, to get a job you either had to start on student films, which were projects being done by film school kids, or you had to know some big shot who worked on the major works in progress. Most of the entry-level jobs were given to people just out of school who had dreams of becoming the next Steven Spielberg or Spike Lee. At twenty-six, I was already old in that world. I had no intention of wasting more precious time running to get coffee for some student. That meant it was more important than ever to make friends with Dayshawn or Grant Pearson and get started in a big way on my new adventure.

I went back down to the first floor and filled out an application for a library card, then found two books to take home with me.

By then, it was rush hour and the Long Island Railroad was packed with weary commuters.

I took a shower and climbed into bed with my books. Nick and I had agreed to order pizza for dinner when he got home from work. I was tired of cooking.

I was reading and then noting pages with important passages when Saundra called.

She was crying so hard, I could barely understand her. My heart started beating rapidly.

"Saundra, calm down and tell me what is going on."

She said something but I only caught the word *Yero.*

"What happened to Yero? Saundra, please, please pull yourself together. I can't understand a word and you're scaring me."

"I'm in the emergency room. Yero . . ."

"Yero what, Saundra?"

"Sick."

More sobs. More moans.

"What is wrong with him?"

That caused a howl from the depths of her soul.

I jumped out of bed. "Where are you?"

"Roosevelt."

There were two hospitals called Roosevelt in Manhattan. One downtown and one near her home in Harlem. I asked anyway just to be sure. "The one on 114th Street?"

"No. Downtown."

Why would she take Yero to an emergency room almost fifty blocks away? She wasn't making sense.

"Stay there. I'm on my way."

"Asha . . ."

"What baby?"

"Yero has . . . oh God, I can't say it."

AIDS! I thought. *My God . . . the man has been frontin' all this time and he isn't some quiet little postal worker. He's been out there fucking around and now both him and my sister have AIDS.*

"Leukemia!"

I was dumbstruck. Horrified. I didn't know a lot about this form of cancer. Only that it acted quickly. It was a death sentence.

"Jesus, Saundra."

"Asha . . . Asha . . . help me," she whimpered.

My heart broke for both of them and the tears began to flow. "I'm on my way, sweetie."

PART TWO

THE DETECTIVE

Chapter 23

SAUNDRA

Imade my way quickly up Tenth Avenue and finally reached Fifty-ninth Street. St. Lukes-Roosevelt took up the whole block. I was carrying a bouquet of red roses for Yero. In just a few weeks, he had lost even more weight. His battle with leukemia sapped most of his strength, but he always seemed a bit perkier when there were flowers in his room.

Asha has been a jewel. She was supposed to join some civic association out where she lives but postponed the whole venture to meet me at the hospital every night when I got off from work. Since Nick got his old job back, he traveled a lot, so Asha spent a lot of nights at my house. Most of the time, I wasn't very good company. I had to interact with people at work, particularly since I was in a new position, but once I left there it was hard for me to make small talk.

So Asha mostly sat around and watched me cry, looked at old pictures of me and Yero, or read books on leukemia and how it can be stopped. Those books had given me a hope that simply did not exist after I heard the diagnosis.

On the days that Asha stayed over, she actually went to the health food emporium, bought stuff that she thought I would like, and cooked it as best she could. She didn't eat any of it herself. Nightime usually found me picking at a salad and a veggie burger while Asha stuffed her face with some dish like pork chops and white rice. The first time Asha surprised me with food from the health food emporium, I was so overcome with emotion that we both ended up hugging each other and crying while the grocery bags sat on the floor. It may seem like a small thing to most people, but Asha has always treated my holistic lifestyle with disdain. Going into the emporium and trying to cook the food properly was an act of love.

Reading the books on this dreadful disease lightened my burden a little. I really believed that Yero was going to live. The real problem was his lack of faith. Studies have shown that people who believe that they're going to get well, actually do get well. I kept telling Yero that over and over again. He pretended to have faith, just so I'd shut up, but he didn't fool me one bit.

The doctors said that Yero had acute leukemia and had to undergo intensive chemotherapy to put it into remission. After that, a bone marrow transplant would be required to replenish the healthy blood cells destroyed by chemotherapy.

Yero was terrified and giving him the books on how to beat it only upset him more. I took them back home.

Asha was scared too.

I kept telling her that this story would have a happy ending, but I saw doubt in her eyes. That's why I hadn't called her in the last three days.

Yero's family was hard enough to deal with. They were totally freaking out . . . like he was going to die or something. His mother is the worst. She was just a walking mound of sadness, and it was really unnerving. The entire Brown family needed to stop sending negative energy out into the universe. But I didn't show my irritation. That would be cruel.

"Yero is a good man," Daddy once said. "Not particularly ambitious but strong and steady. He'll make a good husband."

I walked into the hospital with Daddy's voice ringing in my head. Maybe I should call and tell him what was going on in my life. After all, Yero wasn't mad at him for anything and they were on good terms. Daddy would get these doctors to shape up and fix Yero in a heartbeat.

Yero was propped up in bed wearing a white hospital gown. My hands began to shake when I saw him. His eyes were filled with pain.

A doctor and a nurse were whispering to each other in a corner of the room.

Yero's lips were gray and chapped. I bent over his bed and kissed him.

My eyes welled up.

"Oh, Yero," I said, unable to stop the tears. "Please say you're feeling better."

He squeezed my hand. "Do you really want to cheer me up?"

"Of course, baby. What can I do to make you feel better?"

"Ask Phil to come and see me. I need to hear some of his policeman stories to take my mind off things."

I didn't skip a beat. Even though Daddy and I are on bad terms, up until this moment Yero had not asked for anything and it was good to finally have something concrete that I could do to ease his pain.

"Sure. I'll call Daddy as soon as I get home."

Daddy would be deeply shocked and saddened by what had happened to Yero. After all, Yero and I started dating in high school, so he had watched him grow from adolescence into manhood. They've always gotten along well, and I suspect that Daddy exaggerated his stories of police work because Yero enjoyed his cops-and-robbers tales so much.

He would drop everything that was going on in his life and spend time with my husband.

Chapter 24

PENELOPE

Each month one of the town council members had to act as host or hostess of its monthly meeting. On April 30 it was Penelope Brewster's turn. She and Thelma, who kept a clean home anyway, worked extra hard to buff and polish the place, particularly the living room, until it shone.

"You could have hired a cleaning service just today," Thelma grumbled. They were the only family in the Tremont District who did not have someone to clean at least three times a week.

"I could also fritter away money until you end up in a community college instead or Spelman or Vassar, sweetheart," Penelope replied mildly.

Penelope didn't spend much money on the food either. The menu consisted of Caesar salad, baked chicken, pound cake, and lemonade.

What she did work hard on was her attitude. Since the Hercsville Expansion Project was now a reality, voicing her opposition to the plan was clearly a waste of time. What she wanted to do was get the committee, which would include Asha Seabrook, Shareeka Ellison, and the two actors, Theresa Tanner and Grant Pearson, reporting to her. If she could direct their efforts, there would be many ways to sabotage the initiative and then other citizens of Hercsville would veto the whole idea. So she had to appear sincere, charming, and cooperative. The trees would be saved and Hercsville would remain small and folksy, just as it had always been.

Thelma wasn't on the council and had decided not to be home while the meeting was taking place. When Crenshaw arrived to pick her up, she gave him a dazzling smile, and as they left the house, she managed a friendly wave and told them to have a good time.

Her guests arrived an hour later. When everyone was settled in the living room with plates of food on their laps, she went into her act.

"Everyone, I'd like you to welcome Asha Seabrook, who is seated over there next to the piano in a lovely blue dress, and Shareeka Ellison, who is sitting next to her wearing the stunning brocade pantsuit."

The council members murmured a welcome.

"Ladies, I'd like to introduce you to our members." Penelope gestured as she spoke. "This is Reverend Herbert Best, pastor of the HCS Baptist Church. Mayor Nelson Brown, who has led this town for the past seven years, and Janice Webster, who publishes our town newspaper, the *Hercsville Democrat*, and owns Hercsville Realty. By the way, Janice is also my mother."

Everyone chuckled.

"Asha, we haven't met before today. I'm Dr. Penelope Brewster. I have a mental health practice here in town specializing in children and teens. Do you have any youngsters who need counseling?"

That got another laugh.

Asha smiled and shook her head.

Penelope waved in the direction of a man and woman whose faces were instantly recognizable. They were two of the local celebrities.

"I'm sure that Shareeka is already acquainted with our two other guests since her husband is in show business. So, Asha, please allow me to introduce Grant Pearson and Theresa Tanner, who have so generously volunteered their time and celebrity to help us reach our goal."

Penelope wished that both Asha and the mayor would stop staring at the two entertainers. Starstruck. Both of them. It was disgusting.

At the previous council meeting, the issue of the street signs had been raised again. Penelope spoke to Asha, Shareeka, Grant, and Theresa. "Back in February, Mayor Nelson Brown informed us that our teens want to change a few of the town's street signs. We discussed it briefly at our March meeting, but now it is time to settle this matter. So please bear with us while we clear this up."

"I was never clear about which signs they want to change and what the new names would be," Reverend Best said.

The mayor consulted his notes. "I don't know that they care about which signs are taken down. Their point is that our signs are outdated. They refer to rap musicians who are no longer in vogue. They'd like a few signs to reflect their own times. It is ridiculous that this matter has been on our agenda for three months. All we have to do is throw them a bone. Say that we will replace three signs. It won't cost much to create new ones."

"I say that we leave all the street signs as they are," Janice replied. "Tell them to get their parents to vote for expansion, and when the new streets are built, we'll let them have five names."

"Excellent!" Penelope beamed. "Mayor? Reverend? Do you both agree?"

They did.

Asha looked bored. Shareeka looked angry. Grant and Theresa were whispering to each other.

I don't blame them! Penelope thought angrily. *This whole council meeting is a waste of time! If people don't like the street signs, they should move.*

Penelope turned the meeting over to the mayor. He stood up, stroked his goatee, straightened his tie, and preened in Theresa Tanner's direction until Penelope wanted to punch him in the stomach.

"I have spoken with the governor of New York State and he has agreed to let the Hercsville Expansion Project go forward."

He bowed to the smattering of applause.

What a crock of bullshit! Penelope said to herself. *I don't know who*

Nelson Brown spoke to, but there is no way that he got the governor himself on the phone.

"I just want to say that our governor is a good man who went out of his way to provide me with every courtesy during our very complex negotiations," Nelson said.

He looked directly at Theresa when he said this. She smiled pleasantly.

"So, onward and upward. Our guests here today have generously agreed to become a committee. The purpose of the committee is to do some public relations. In other words, inform the other citizens of Hercsville and get them to agree that the town's expansion is a good idea."

He paused, took a sip of lemonade, and spoke directly to Theresa. "Miss Tanner, would you be good enough to head the committee?"

Penelope and her mother exchanged irritated glances. Nelson was really making a prize ass out of himself.

Theresa spoke simply. "I don't think that is a good idea because I never know when I'll have to leave town. Right now I'm between roles, but if my agent needs me to leave for Hollywood, I'd have to go. Then the committee would be left without a leader."

Grant swallowed a mouthful of chicken and agreed. "Same goes for me."

The mayor fixed his gaze on Asha and Shareeka. "Ladies, would either of you like to volunteer?"

Asha's hand shot up. "I would."

It was clear from the adoring glances that Asha had been giving Grant all afternoon that she was only taking on the huge task so that she would have a reason to contact him. Penelope was ready to puke.

Nelson clapped his hands together. "Excellent. So we now have our committee, which will be led by Asha Seabrook. The other committee members are Grant Pearson, Theresa Tanner, and Shareeka Ellison."

Why did he have to repeat what they'd all just heard? Penelope fumed. Did he think that everyone in the room suffered from attention deficit disorder?

"Let's move on, Nelson," Janice said tartly. "Asha, you will need to keep in touch with Reverend Best. He will direct your efforts and bring any concerns that you may have directly to us."

It was the moment that Penelope had been waiting for. "Mama, I think that Reverend Best has enough to do just keeping the congregation of HCS Baptist Church together. I have plenty of spare time."

Reverend Best chimed in. "Thank you, Dr. Penny, but I accept Janice's offer. It will give me a chance to get out in the community and meet people who have not yet joined our church."

Penelope fixed him with an evil stare. "Didn't you mention something a few meetings ago about raising money for poor children?"

The reverend blinked rapidly in confusion. He was unsure what to make of her hostility. "What has that got to do with the project we're talking about?"

"Isn't that what ministers are supposed to do? Help poor people?"

Janice was clearly astonished. "Penelope, what on earth has gotten into you?"

Penelope composed herself and remembered that you could catch more flies with honey than you ever could with a jar of vinegar. She chuckled ruefully. "I'm sorry, Reverend. It's just that I drove through Flash Place yesterday and I was quite overcome by the suffering of some of Hercsville's neediest citizens."

Grant sighed. "I can understand that. In fact, why can't we figure out a way to help them? I mean, the expansion project is a big deal but we can handle more than one thing at a time."

Reverend Best glowered at Penelope.

The four guests were riveted to the drama unfolding before them like it was a TV show.

"That is exactly what I mean," Penelope said carefully, realizing that thanks to Grant and his celebrity, she actually had a chance of winning the argument.

Janice wiped her hands on a napkin and cleared her throat. "Maybe we should take a vote."

"Good," Penelope said brightly. "But first, I need to clear away some of these dishes and bring in the dessert. Reverend Best, would you be good enough to help me?"

What could he do except gather plates and follow her into the kitchen? It was there that she turned on him with a fury.

"What do you think you're doing?"

"Dr. Penny, do you mind telling me what is going on?"

"What is going on is that you won't be able to keep that hellcat Shareeka Ellison in line. I know that woman very well. She told me herself that if they have their way, we will have rap music nightclubs springing up all over town." Penelope told this lie without batting an eyelash. "She will use her husband's celebrity to change this town to fit her own needs. Of course, you had no way of knowing that, but you should have thrown in the towel when I insisted on leading the committee. You should have known that I had a good reason. Now you've embarrassed me in front of everyone. I want an apology."

"Well . . . sure, Dr. Penny. Like you say, how would I know anything about plans for a rap club?"

"Good." Penelope patted him on the shoulder. "Now, I know that you've wanted the council to come up with a plan to help the poor children of Flash Place. Put together a proposal before the next meeting and I promise to back it all the way at the next meeting. Do we have a deal?"

They had a deal.

Chapter 25

NANCY

Nancy Rosa St. Bart gazed in anger at her man, Bruce Benedict. He perched on the edge of her couch watching *Desperate Housewives* while munching happily on buffalo chicken wings and celery sticks. Every once in a while, he took a sip from the bottle of beer on the coffee table in front of him. He was immaculately dressed as always. The black shirt was starched and the black jeans were dry-cleaned and creased within an inch of their cottony lives. His mighty shoulders rumbled every time he reached for the beer.

An outsider would gaze upon his handsome face and guess that Bruce was no older than thirty, but he was just past his forty-fifth birthday. Nancy glowered at him from the doorway.

"I'm turning in," she declared.

Bruce turned around and gave her a dazzling smile. He had perfect teeth. "All right. Sleep well."

Nancy was pissed. Again. What was this? The hundredth time she was going to sleep alone? Did Bruce have another woman? Was Bruce turned off by her physically for some reason? What was going on? How long was she supposed to tolerate it?

She stormed upstairs, slammed the bedroom door, snatched the fluffy pink slippers from her feet, and plopped herself onto the queen-sized bed. It was nine o'clock on a Sunday night and she had to be on the set of *The Bridesmaid* before sunrise. She had been late twice the week before, and now the director was threatening to replace her.

She had always liked that Bruce, whom she considered a brilliant and perceptive comic, had seen past the thick black eyebrows and the stereotype of the overweight, sassy black female to the vulnerable and sensitive woman she actually was.

Unfortunately, Bruce's keen observations stopped right there. Otherwise, he would have his black ass in bed with her instead of down in the living room watching TV.

She knew that Bruce would pull out the sofa bed when he was ready to sleep. That's what he had been doing lately. She hadn't asked him why. She was afraid to know the answer.

Nancy was truly furious. It was now the first of April and they hadn't made love in weeks. She had thrown hints and tried to hold him during the nights when he did come up to bed. All to no avail. Now his message was real clear. He didn't find her attractive anymore. Fine! Years of loneliness between boyfriends had taught Nancy how to please herself.

Nancy's heavy thighs parted. A framed full-length color poster of Denzel Washington hung on the wall in front of the bed, and she fixed her eyes on his lips now . . . as she did every night. Her left hand slid the nightgown up past her belly button. The index finger of her right hand lightly rubbed her clitoris. Her hips moved in an ancient rhythm meant for two and her breath became ragged. Finally, her fingers were soaked and a low moan escaped from her lips.

Nancy fell asleep, happy that Denzel was spending the night with her . . . again.

The pink phone on the nightstand rang and she turned away from it in her sleep. In this dream, Denzel was kicking Bruce's short, bald ass from one side of a huge banquet hall to the other.

"Nancy keeps a roof over your head, food in your stomach, and lets you use her contacts to showcase your comedy routine," Denzel complained. "Don't you know what sexual rejection does to a woman's spirit? Her self-esteem? This is the way you repay her?"

Bruce replied with a ringing moan that seemed to come from way down in his soul.

It was the phone.

It was a quarter to four in the morning. It must be the mysterious caller. She could feel herself getting hot with anger as she picked up the receiver.

"Hello?"

"Is this Nancy?" It was that same female voice.

"I'm not starting up with this crazy shit again."

"Oh, yes, you are," the woman replied cheerfully.

"How did you get my new phone number?"

"Aw, come on, Nancy. Did you really think that a new number would solve your problems? That move was tired. Real tired."

"I'm hanging up."

"That's what I was going to suggest."

"Huh?"

"Look on your doorstep. I left you a message."

There was a click. The woman was gone.

Nancy got out of bed, jammed her feet into her slippers, and headed downstairs, screaming for Bruce the whole time.

Her shouts woke him up. He sat on the edge of the sofa in a pair of blue cotton boxer shorts, rubbing his eyes and staring at her in alarm. "What's the matter, baby?"

"Baby! If I'm your damn baby, why are you sleeping down here?"

He looked annoyed. "You come screaming in here like the house is on fire to ask me that?"

Nancy ran a hand across the silk scarf that covered her hair. "Open the front door."

"What?"

"Remember that scary woman I told you about?"

He nodded, looking deeply concerned. "The one who was making threatening phone calls to you?"

"Yeah. She just called again. Said she left something on the doorstep for me. I'm scared to go look."

Bruce turned on the lights and pulled on his bathrobe.

At first, she'd planned to leave Bruce in the dark about the whole affair. But after Shareeka got tired of hearing about it, she needed a fresh ear. Besides, he had been very suspicious when she changed the number. Something was definitely wrong in their relationship and it could not stand the strain of his distrust. She was not cheating on him. He had listened carefully and then told her it was probably some nasty prank by some bored teenager.

He headed for the door with her on his tail.

"Nancy, do any teenagers live in that house across the road?"

Nancy thought hard. "I don't think so. Why?"

He turned around and grinned. "If some kid is watching our front door, they're going to crack up laughing when they see us outside in our robes."

Shareeka's frown disappeared. She sighed with relief.

Bruce opened the door.

"Aarggh!" he shrieked and backed up. "Call the police!"

"What is it?"

He just stood there, looking down.

Nancy pushed him aside and suddenly felt ill.

A dead puppy lay on its side. Its throat had been cut. Blood was pouring from the wound.

There was a photo in its mouth.

Nancy screamed and screamed and screamed.

A week later, Nancy dragged herself up Fifth Avenue, trying to remember the name of the restaurant where her agent, Eric Collins, was waiting for her. She felt exhausted. It was her first time out of the house since the dog incident.

The cops had been no help at all. They called the ASPCA, who showed up asking dozens of inane questions. One cop had kept eyeing Bruce suspiciously. Could he have something to do with all this? She had once seen a movie in which a husband kept pulling evil pranks to drive his wife crazy so he could control her inheritance. But she and Bruce weren't married, and if something were to happen to her, he would be homeless because Mama and Randall were her closest living relatives. They would throw his ass out and seize her bank account before even planning her funeral. Bruce knew that. Therefore, he had everything to lose if she went crazy or died.

Bruce didn't have anything to do with this evil. Her tormentor was still out there somewhere.

She brushed away a tear, feeling totally despondent.

She had been going over some bills last night when Eric Collins had called.

"We need to talk as soon as possible. I've got good news and bad news. How about lunch tomorrow?"

"I have to work. I've been sick all week. I don't dare push my luck," she replied.

"They don't need you on the set tomorrow."

"That's not true," Nancy said, beginning to get scared.

"Yes, it is. I'm sorry. That's the bad news."

When Nancy put the phone down, she knew that the producers of *The Bridesmaid* had fired her, but Eric was saving his "good news" for tomorrow.

Now she pushed her way through the crowded Manhattan streets, made a left turn onto Avenue of the Americas, and entered a restaurant that sat on the corner of Fifty-seventh Street. She blinked rapidly until her eyes adjusted to the dim light.

Eric, a black-haired Irishman with bright, blue eyes, was sipping a cranberry juice and seltzer. He stood up when she reached the table.

"It's good to see you, Eric."

They cheek-kissed and Nancy wondered bitterly why she had become an actress instead of an agent. Eric, who was in his late twenties, looked unruffled and prosperous.

Nancy sat down. "Please give me the good news, Eric."

Eric smiled. "How would you like to do a series of Fab Floor Shine commercials?"

"I bet they want a fat, black woman who can fake a southern accent or a ghetto accent to sell their stupid cleaner."

"Nancy, *The Bridesmaid* is over. Let's talk to these Fab Floor Shine folks and see what they want. I'll tell you this, they asked for you in particular. So you don't have to fight a bunch of other actresses to get the gig. Plus, they're offering a lot of money."

"Why was I fired? Because of lateness?"

"No. They simply wrote your character out of the plot. It wasn't personal."

"The cowardly bastards could have told me to my face."

Eric shrugged. "That's show biz."

Nancy started sobbing. "Bruce is on the couch. Dead, bleeding dogs are on my doorstep and now I have no job. It's all too much."

Eric looked at her in alarm. "Dead dogs? What are you talking about?"

The waiter came to take their order, but Eric waved him away.

Nancy sobbed louder. "This woman called. She threatened to kill me and Bruce. No, first she was going to kill Mama and Randall but—"

"Whoa! Slow down. Start from the beginning."

Nancy started with the first phone call and filled him in. By the time she finished, Eric's blue eyes were the size of saucers.

"You need a private investigator to get to the bottom of this extremely dangerous situation." He pulled out his cell phone and dialed a number. "I'm calling my lawyer. He'll get someone right on it."

"Wait," Nancy protested. "How am I going to pay for this?"

"Fab Floor Shine," Eric answered grimly.

Chapter 26

ED

Keith Williams was a world-famous African-American defense attorney. He did some pro bono work, but the majority of his clients were high-level executives, society types, or well-paid singers and other artists. Long before I started working for him as a private detective, he had defended a white soap opera star who was accused of shooting her real-life mother seventeen times in the head. The evidence of guilt was overwhelming and she was facing death by lethal injection, but Keith dazzled the jury and she walked out of that courtroom a free woman. He had won other high-profile cases as well: a book publishing executive accused of murdering her boss in a Park Avenue bathroom, and Lawbreaker, a Grammy award winning–rapper in a sensational trial with a completely ridiculous foundation. The musician had allegedly beat his valet to death with a baseball bat just for trash-talking him.

I used to be a cop. In fact, I was the arresting officer on the Lawbreaker case. That's how I met Keith. Even though my side lost, he admired the extra time and attention that I'd put into the whole affair. In fact, that case was one of the reasons why I got promoted to detective just a few years later. He and I remained friends, and when I quit the force after completing a particularly gruesome case, he offered me a job. I like working for his law firm because he is a nice guy who only takes cases that offer some sort of mental challenge, and the perks are top-notch.

Our offices are in Trump Tower over on Fifth Avenue in Manhattan. Walking into the reception area, you'd probably think that it was the home of a private group of super-rich investment bankers. The man spared no expense when it came to interior decoration. While his office is done up in white carpet, white silk wallpaper, silver lamps, and glass furniture, mine is far more low-key. I have a desk with a computer and phone on it. A bookcase and two extra chairs. The color scheme is beige and burgundy just like his reception area.

He buzzed my extension, and while he talked, I pictured him sitting behind the glass desk: He was in his late thirties, light-skinned with a clear complexion and close-cropped hair. His eyes blazed through you and missed nothing.

"Ed, how much do you have on your plate?"

"Not a whole lot," I admitted.

Keith knew that. I'd just wrapped up my investigation into a credit card scam run by a spoiled rich brat in his midtwenties. The family hired us to get the details, negotiate a quiet deal with the district attorney, and keep the whole mess out of the papers.

"I need you to run out to Long Island and talk to a woman named Nancy Rosa St. Bart."

"What's her problem?"

"I'm not sure. She's an actress and somebody is threatening her. In fact, they left a dead dog on her front steps."

"Is she a sister?"

"Yeah. She works on a soap opera."

Soap opera players don't make a lot of money unless they have the starring roles, and I'd never heard of the woman. "This pro bono?"

"No. She can afford us up to about ten thousand dollars. After that, we'll have to talk."

"At four hundred an hour, it won't take long. Why did you take her on?"

"She didn't call me. Eric Collins did."

Eric Collins had been Keith's client and a good friend for a long time.

"Okay. I'll need her address and phone number."

"Let me know what happens."

This sounded like a piece-of-shit case to me, but Keith was the boss, so I wrote down the information and started working.

The first step was a Google search. Her name only generated seventy-five hits. I read through all of them and studied her picture, which appeared on a Web site that was dedicated to the show she worked on. It was called *The Bridesmaid*. She played the hairdresser: a wisecracking, hefty black woman with a heart of gold. In an interview that she'd given to *Soap Opera Weekly* a few years before, she said that she was born and raised in New York, was divorced, and had no children. Her hobbies were reading Victorian literature and watching old movies. Her favorite color was blue.

Unless she was sleeping with one of her famous costars and he murdered the poor dog, this case sounded like a snooze.

A man answered on the first ring. I asked to speak to her without giving my name or affiliation. She came to the phone, sounding slightly out of breath.

"This is Nancy."

I explained my reason for calling.

"Did Eric tell you about Fab Floor Shine?"

"That mop and glow stuff?"

"I think it is a product like that, yes."

"No. Why don't you fill me in?"

"It's just that I can't pay you until they pay me and we haven't even filmed the first TV commercial yet."

"Oh. I don't get involved with the contracts and money, but I will mention it to my boss. My job is to find out who is tormenting you. When can I stop by your house so we can talk?"

"Well, since I'm unemployed now, just come over whenever you want."

It was almost noon.

"How about right now?"

"Fine."

I wondered who the man was who had answered the phone. Did he kill the animal? She mentioned unemployment. Had she killed the dog herself just to get publicity?

I breezed through the Queens Midtown Tunnel in a five-year-old dented brown station wagon that I only used for work. In my line of work, it was important to blend in and not attract attention. It was the first week of May, and as I drove through suburbia, I noticed that the trees and flowers were in bloom. The grass and shrubs were a beautiful green. I had hoped to have a house of my own on Long Island by now with a loving wife and two beautiful kids living in it with me. But I was quickly approaching my fortieth birthday and the woman I'd been seeing for the past two years seemed less and less into me. We were having dinner later on that night. She said that there was something important she had to talk to me about. Was she going to dump me like all the others had?

The town of Hercsville turned out to be a gated community. A security guard in the booth looked closely at my ID, wrote down my license plate number, and called Nancy, who gave the go-ahead to let me through. An enormous black gate swung open in front of me. So it was not possible to just drive up to Nancy's door and drop something. You had to come through a security system. Either the sicko lived in town or was visiting someone who did.

I got lost a few times and had to flag down patrol cars and private vehicles for directions. The district and community names made me laugh. Who founded this damned town, anyway? An aging hip-hopper? I'd check that out after the interview.

Nancy's house was painted white. I parked the car and knocked. She opened the door and I was surprised at how pretty she was. The Internet photos definitely didn't do her justice. She was wearing a pink sleeveless dress with matching sandals and no makeup.

"I'm Ed Winsome."

She held out a hand but did not smile. "I'm Nancy. Come on in."

I followed her through the foyer, living room, and dining room. By the time we reached the kitchen, I had decided that my new client was as crazy as they come. Every single wall was papered with photos of Denzel Washington to the point where it was impossible to tell what color the paint was underneath. To make matters worse, Mo Better Blues was playing on a big-screen TV in the living room. The volume was turned off. I've seen some crazy shit in my line of work, but this was way over the top.

There was too much furniture in each room, but all of it was attractive, in a very masculine way. All of it was expensive.

There was a man sitting at the kitchen table. He stood up and shook my hand. "I'm Bruce Benedict," he said. He watched my reaction closely as though his name should be familiar to me. It wasn't.

The three of us sat at the table. Yes, even in the kitchen, Denzel ruled. I pulled out a pad and pen.

She was clearly depressed. Her shoulders sagged and she kept her eyes down. Clearly neither of them was going to say anything, so I had to break the ice.

"So why am I here?"

Nancy looked at Bruce. "Why don't you tell him? I'm tired of telling this story."

Bruce patted her on the back. "My lady has been getting weird phone calls that scare her half to death. You're here because it has gone too far. The dog is the last straw."

"It is a very difficult situation for both of you. The dog must have been a horrible shock, but it is important for me to hear every single word that the caller said."

She talked while Bruce got up and made coffee.

Afterward, I mulled the information over.

"The woman said that you had a chance to save her but you didn't. Did you ever leave the scene of an accident, refuse to give blood to a sick friend, decline to testify in court for the victim of a crime? Anything like that?"

She shook her head from side to side.

No.

"What about something less dramatic? Maybe someone was in danger of losing her job because of something you didn't do. You knew the truth but didn't speak up."

"I never had a chance to save anybody from anything."

"Someone thinks you did."

That truth hung in the air, oppressing the three of us.

Bruce looked at me. He was a short, stocky man who was dressed completely in black. Black shirt. Black jeans. Black loafers.

"Do you take it with cream?"

"Thanks, man, but I don't drink coffee. Some ice water would be great, though."

When we had our coffees and water, I gestured at the wall. "Why so much Denzel?"

Nancy perked up instantly. "He's casting a new movie here in New York soon. Eric has promised to get me a reading."

I managed a grin and chose my next words carefully. "Are you hoping that all these pictures will bring you luck?"

She laughed. "No. Nothing like that, although it's not a bad idea."

She didn't volunteer anything more and Bruce suddenly looked pissed off, so I let it go. For now.

"Can you think of anyone who would want to harm you for any reason?"

A look passed between them.

Bruce stood up. "Well, it was nice meeting you, Mr. Winsome. I'm going to let you two handle your business."

We shook hands and he left the room. I could hear his footsteps as he went upstairs.

Nancy whispered, "I had an affair a while back. The man's wife is named Ivie. She harassed us long after it was over."

"How long ago was this?"

"Two years."

"Would you recognize Ivie's voice if you heard it again?"

"Sure. She had a southern accent. It definitely wasn't Ivie who called me recently. I figure she got one of her girlfriends to do it. The only thing I can't figure out is how she knows so much about my mother and brother. Vernon, her husband, and I never talked about my family."

"The caller said that your mother was a coward and your brother, a dumb-ass. I take it you agree?"

"Oh no! I come from a very close-knit family."

"You can be close to your relatives and still think they're cowards or dumb-asses."

She giggled. "You're funny."

"I have a cousin named Richie who is a total loser but I love him to death."

"Well, since you put it like that . . . maybe you're right. The caller was right."

"Good. Now, tell me about you and Bruce. Is he your husband?"

"No. We just live together. He's a comedian. In fact, he is performing in Manhattan next week. You should come."

Ah! That's why he thought I should recognize his name.

"Maybe I will. Nancy, someone out there doesn't like you. Bruce is right when he says that that someone has now gone too far. So let's put our heads together right now and make a list of everyone that you don't like or who doesn't like you. That makes sense, right?"

She frowned in concentration. "Besides Ivie?"

"Yes, aside from Ivie. By the way, I'll need the contact information for both her and Vernon before I leave."

She groaned. "Please don't stir up that old mess again."

"Nancy, you told me there was blood spilled on your doorstep. Doesn't that scare you?"

"Yes. As a matter of fact, I told Bruce that he can't take any more out-of-town gigs until all this is over. I don't want to be alone at night."

"How does he feel about that?"

"He agreed with me but I know it bothers him. Struggling comedians need to leave whenever somebody is willing to put them onstage."

"Does Bruce have any other income?"

"No, and a lot of times he doesn't even get paid to work these showcases, but that's how it is when you're trying to make it."

So Bruce was living off her. Deep down inside, he had to resent that.

"You mentioned unemployment. Is your show going off the air?"

She went on a ten-minute rant about the unfairness of the producers and how embarrassing it was going to be hawking floor cleaner.

We weren't getting anywhere.

"Nancy, since you can't come up with any enemies, tell me about your friends. Who are they and what do they do for a living?"

She brightened. "I have a lot of associates but not many people that I really call friends. My main girl lives right here in town. Her name is Shareeka Ellison. She never had a job. Her husband is Dayshawn Ellison."

"The movie guy?"

"Yes. Do you like his work?"

Actually I didn't like the middle-of-the-road pap that he was putting out lately, but it wouldn't do me any good to say so.

"Yeah. He is one talented brother. It's amazing how he reinvented himself after all those years doing gangsta rap."

She beamed. "Yeah. He's a great guy. They've got two kids. A boy and a girl. If you meet Dayshawn, don't call him Bustacap. He hates that."

I had to laugh at that one. "I don't blame him."

"You're not wearing a wedding ring."

"I'm not married."

"Why not? You're a good-looking guy with an interesting job."

She wasn't flirting with me. It was clear that Nancy was just a woman who liked saying what was on her mind.

"No. The woman I wanted to marry didn't like the idea of being married to a cop. Back then, I was in uniform walking a beat in Harlem. I guess she was afraid of becoming a young widow."

She looked thoughtful. "I was married once."

"Where is your ex-husband?"

"Last I heard, he was living in Canada. That's where he was from. When we busted up, he went back home."

"Are you still friends?"

"We don't keep in touch."

"Maybe he's still angry . . . enough to get a woman to make threatening calls to you."

"No. That and the dead animal require a lot of work. My ex-husband was afraid of work. That's why we're not together."

Oh. The woman had a history of getting pimped. Interesting.

I looked at my notes. "So far, we have Shareeka and her husband. We have Bruce. We have your ex. Plus Vernon and Ivie."

"Ivie is the only one capable of this. She threatened to stab me to death if I didn't stay away from her husband."

"When is the last time you saw him?"

She looked me dead in the eye. "We're not fucking around anymore."

That was clear enough.

I stood up. "Nancy, I'm going to the police department and review their notes on the dog incident. Then I'm going to talk to all the people you've mentioned. In the meantime, I want you to make some lists for me. One list of friends of either sex. One list of ex-lovers. A list of jealous or angry show business folks."

There was a noise. It sounded like jangling keys.

"What was that?"

She shrugged. "Just the cleaning lady. Actually, I should say cleaning girl because she's only twenty years old. She comes in three times a week."

"What is her name?"

"Jaleesa, but don't go bothering her. We haven't known each other long enough for her to hate me."

Chapter 27

SHAREEKA

Shareeka listened with her mouth opened as Nancy told her about Ed's visit and his upcoming investigation. When it was over, Shareeka stood up and looked down at her friend who was still reclining on the couch.

"Gurl, you need a good stiff drink."

"Right." Nancy smiled at Shareeka. "I'll have Bacardi on the rocks."

"A Corona for me, thanks."

"Punk."

Shareeka waved away the insult. "Someone has to keep a clear head while we figure out who this bitch is."

"Maybe it's just a mean, spiteful prank and there is no real danger at all."

"Stop talking crazy, Nancy."

"I've made the lists that Ed asked for, but when I read them, no name jumped out at me."

"Did Bruce read the lists, too?"

"I can't ask him to. As soon as I mention Ivie, it just stirs up a bunch of old shit that I don't want to deal with. We're barely on solid ground as it is."

Shareeka's bar was on the far side of her living room. She got their drinks and they both took several swallows.

"Nancy, I know you want to believe that you can't get killed in this mess, but you've got to stop that shit right now. This is war, Nancy. Bruce needs to watch his back, too."

"I have an idea."

"What?"

"The next time she calls, I'm going to curse her out."

"That'll scare her," Stephanie said dryly.

Nancy laughed. "What I mean is that I'm going to force her hand. She says I've got thirty days to guess who she is and I'll say fuck you. If this is a serious threat, she'll have to do something dramatic to get my attention again."

"Dramatic as in kill your mama?"

Nancy frowned. "Do you have a solution?"

"I say you make a list of every female you hate. Chances are that they dislike you also."

"Hate? That's a pretty strong word. There are people I'd rather not work with or have over for dinner . . . but there isn't anybody I hate."

Shareeka thought for a moment. "Fine. How about a list of everyone, male or female, that you've had a disagreement with in your whole life?"

Nancy liked that one better. "Okay. Starting from birth. Damn, I'll be typing all night. By the way, Ed Winsome wants to talk to all my friends. Is that all right?"

"Sure, tell Ed that he can come see me any time he wants. This is some crazy shit. I'm real worried about you. Why don't you come stay here with us until he catches this crazy bitch?"

"Well . . . I dunno . . . who knows how long it's gonna take?"

"Who cares how long it takes? That way, Bruce can go do his thing and I'll have company when the kids go to sleep."

"I'm not letting anybody run me out of my own house."

"Then at least borrow one of Dayshawn's guns. Next time she shows up lugging a dog, you put a cap in her ass."

Nancy laughed. "I don't know how to shoot a gun."

"Fuck that shit. I'll tell Dayshawn to give you a lesson."

She changed the subject. "How are things going between you two?"

"Good. I joined this group that's trying to make Hercsville a bigger town, and that made him happy. The only reason I did it was so he could stop bitchin' about how I'm not even tryin' to fit in around here."

Nancy shook almost half a bottle of hot sauce onto her meal. "That sounds boring as hell."

"Girl, it is. Guess who I saw there?"

"Who?"

"Asha. That female that ran into my car with her half-driving ass."

"Oh. How is she doing?"

"All right. We talked after the meeting. I like her. She's real cool."

"Yeah. She seemed okay."

"I told her to come see me. It gets boring just wandering around this house. She's the type that always got somethin' goin' on. I need somebody like that around."

"Is she coming to your party?"

"Nancy, nobody is coming to Dayshawn's birthday party except people from back in the day."

"So I'm not invited?"

I put my hand on hers. "Please don't get mad, gurl."

She laughed and punched me on the arm. "What if I'm living here . . . hiding out from a dog killer? What do I have to do? Stay in my room?"

There was nothing funny about my need to go home. "Maybe you could take the kids and go see a play in the city."

"You serious?"

"Serious as sickle cell."

Chapter 28

ASHA

When we were dating, Nick bought me a silver STS V-8 Cadillac with a Bose 5.1 studio surround-sound system. I kept it in a garage most of the time. On the one occasion that I parked it on the street in front of my apartment house, somebody stole it. That was right before my wedding and I hadn't had my own car since then. Here in Hercsville, I used the cab service when Nick had to take the Mercedes.

I was tired of it.

He was crisscrossing the country these days, checking up on the managers who were in charge of the day-to-day operations at the Seabrook Soul Food restaurants. I hated to jump on him with a complaint as soon as he walked in the door, but I needed my own wheels. What bugged me even more was that I didn't have the means to buy my own car because I didn't have a job. I used to dream about not having to work, and now that I had that lifestyle, it made me feel scared and insecure.

Another human being bought me food, kept a roof over my head, and put clothes on my back. That same human being could flip on me tomorrow and decide not to do those things. True, I socked a lot of money away while I was single, but that is for my old age. I refuse to end up old and poor.

So, aside from the car, I also needed a job.

That's where Shareeka Ellison came in. I put the bug in her ear after the last council meeting and she promised to talk to her husband. She's a real nice lady. Not many people would be so generous to somebody they just met. I also think that she is lonely. Just like me.

So I spent a lot of time at her house playing cards and watching videos. I never get tired of watching The Gangbangers. Or of Cheery. She reminds me a lot of myself when I was a little girl. Like Cheery, I had to be my mother's confidante. Listen to her problems; massage her back with my little hands. Tell her that everything was going to be all right. It's too much responsibility for a little girl, and I wanted to talk to Shareeka about it. Maybe I would. After she got me a job.

In the meantime, I needed to find some way to make this marriage work. How could I get Nick to see me as his girlfriend again? I've seen women struggling with this same problem in a lot of TV movies, but it usually doesn't happen so soon after the wedding date. Those women do desperate things like greeting their husbands at the door, draped in see-through cellophane. Of course, it doesn't work and they end up hurt and humiliated. I'm not going out like that.

Maybe if I acted like the old Asha, he'd start acting like the old Nick.

Who was the old Asha?

A party girl.

A clotheshorse.

An on-the-go woman who didn't take no shit.

You can't be any of those things without money.

I decided to call Shareeka and give her a nudge.

"Hey, Shareeka."

"What's up, gurl?"

"I'm going crazy sitting here in this house. Did you get a chance to talk to Dayshawn yet? I need a job real bad."

"He's in town tonight. Why don't you come on over and talk to him yourself? Bring your bathing suit. We'll be out by the pool."

"Now? At night?"

"Our pool area is lighted and the water is heated. Come on over. We'll have a great time."

"Give me ten minutes. Thanks, Shareeka."

"Anytime, gurl."

Half an hour later, I buzzed the button at the intercom next to the golden gate that surrounded Shareeka's house.

"Yes?" Shareeka asked.

"It's Asha."

"Okay."

The gates opened and as I walked up the winding cobble-stoned pathway toward the house, I lifted my large shades in complete awe once again at their gorgeous Spanish-style mansion. The towering pastel pink and gold palace was surrounded by lush greenery, a tree house, and marigolds strategically planted in a zigzag pattern. It was tacky but it reflected Shareeka's horrible street interpretation of what was "classy."

"Hey, gurl!" Shareeka said, walking toward me in a black one-piece bathing suit and an oversized sarong that attempted to masquerade her love handles.

"Hey!" I said, kissing the air on both sides of her face.

"Did you remember your bathing suit? I set up everything near the pool so we can kick it."

"I sure did."

Shareeka smiled. "Good."

Dayshawn was standing behind her. "Hi, Asha, nice to see you again."

"Nice to see you too, Dayshawn, will you be hanging with us?"

"Maybe just for a minute, I know you two want to talk girl talk."

Shareeka smiled. "Yup."

I brushed up against him by accident as she entered the house.

"Dayshawn, take Asha to the pool while I bring out some snacks."

He nodded his head. "This way."

We passed through their living room, which was almost an exact replica of Tony Montana's from *Scarface*, including the gawdy fountain that made absolutely no sense.

"I see somebody is a fan of the movies," I said, jerking my head toward the fountain.

Dayshawn put his hands in his pockets shyly. "Yeah, I used to watch *Scarface* like every day when I was younger. I remember when I was a kid I said if I ever got rich I'd have a fountain in the house just like him."

"I see."

"Now I'm over it, though, but Shareeka would kill me if I got rid of it. She loves that thing. Do you like it?"

He slid open the glass doors leading out to the dollar-sign-shaped pool and I frowned. The whole place needed to be de-ghettoized.

"To be honest with you, I don't, but don't mind me, I'm kind of a square when it comes to home furnishings. I guess I'm conservative in that area."

"No offense taken, I'm actually getting to be the same way. Like this pool . . . I dunno."

"*Scarface* again?"

He laughed. "No, Shareeka designed it. There was no dollar-sign-shaped pool in *Scarface.* Didn't you see it?"

"Yeah, a long time ago. It was a great movie, but I never understood the obsession with Tony by all these kids."

Dayshawn looked puzzled. "Because he was cool!"

I shook my head. "Not to me. Sosa was the one who should be imitated, if anybody. Sosa was the winner, so why all the celebration for the loser? I guess people will always follow brawn instead of brains."

"Huh. I guess I never thought of it that way."

I winked. "Still waters run deep."

Shareeka slid open the door while balancing a tray of buffalo wings. "I hope you're hungry, these wings are the shit."

"They smell great," I said as I removed my off-the-shoulder sundress that covered a skimpy bronze bikini. Out the corner of my eye, I saw Dayshawn's mouth open slightly.

"Look at those abs! You must not eat anything," Shareeka said, placing the wings on the table.

"Actually, I can eat anything and not gain a pound. I get that from my father's side of the family. My dad would put so much food on his plate you couldn't even see the rim, but he was thin as a rail. At least that's what my mother always told me."

"Wow, I wish I could do that. I know these wings are going straight to my thighs, but life is short."

"I agree, you should enjoy yourself. I wish I could gain weight." I sighed sadly and lay back on the beach chair.

Shareeka smiled awkwardly. "No, girl, you look great."

"Thanks."

"All right, ladies, I'm gonna be going now. You two have a good time."

Dayshawn stood up but Shareeka pulled him back by the hand. "Stay and have something to eat. Cheery and Crenshaw are bringing the rest of the food in a minute. Besides, I need you to do Asha a favor."

He looked at me and grinned. "Whasssup?"

"I'm a production assistant but I'm out of work right now. Do you have anything coming up that I could work on?"

He was facing me with his back to Shareeka. His eyes roamed over my body. "Most definitely."

Shareeka clapped her hands and grabbed him around the waist. "Good! Which project is it?"

He winked at me and then turned to his wife. "I've got a couple of things going. But listen, I've got to leave you ladies to eat that food. It's time for me to take off."

"Where are you going?"

"I told you about that drink thing in the city with Jerry Seinfeld and his wife. You didn't want to go. Remember?"

"Okay, honey, see you later. What time will you be home?"

"Not late, I'll call you."

He gave Shareeka a smooch on the lips. I was lying on a deck chair. I took out some oil and generously applied it to my arms and legs. I knew that I looked like a shimmering goddess in the lights they had strung around the pool area.

"Take care, Dayshawn," I said, waving.

Dayshawn looked over his shoulder at me. "Shareeka will give you my cell number. Call me tomorrow." He walked back through the glass doors.

"I am so glad you came over or he would have jumped on my ass about not going with him this evening," Shareeka said, waving her hand as she sat in the chair next to me.

"Why?"

"Dayshawn wants me to be all up in those folks' face just 'cause he likes them. I swear I dunno how that stupid-ass Seinfeld muthafucka got his own show when he ain't even funny."

"Oh, come on, Shareeka! That show was hilarious."

"I don't know any black people besides you and Dayshawn that think that shit is funny."

"Yeah, I know a lot of our folks didn't like that show, but I did. But to be fair, a lot of people that didn't live in New York City didn't get the show either because a lot of the jokes were real specific to New Yorkers."

Shareeka stared blankly. "I guess. So how is Nick?"

"Oh, he's fine. His mother is coming to visit tomorrow and I'm not looking forward to that at all."

Shareeka laughed. "Is she a pain in the ass or you just don't feel like smiling and nodding at her suggestions like you give a fuck?"

"Exactly. Nick's mother thinks she knows everything, and she's old enough to know she should keep her opinions to herself. Sometimes I swear she thinks he's still in Oshkosh."

"I hope I'm not like that when my kids get grown."

"You will be."

Shareeka chuckled. "Oh no, I won't! If I don't like the girl Crenshaw is with I'll just slap that ho!"

"Does Dayshawn's mother like you?"

"Yeah, she loves me. But she says it was because of me that Dayshawn never went to college. If he woulda done that, he wouldn't ever have been Bustacap and her ungrateful ass wouldn't be living in a minimansion right about now."

"That's true."

"She also thinks I got pregnant with Crenshaw to put Dayshawn on lock."

"Did you?"

Shareeka threw back her head and let out a hearty laugh. "Gurl, you a mess. You goddamn right, I did. Fans and groupies and all kinds of bitches were offering him ass on the regular. I had to clear that shit up. But I love my mother-in-law and she treats me like a daughter."

That was funny. "I don't blame you one bit for getting pregnant," I chuckled. "I would have done the exact same thing."

Shareeka sucked her teeth. "Now he likes runnin' around with all these white folks. He used to hate all those stuffy people and those events he had to go to, but now he enjoys that shit. What's even worse is he wants me to like it too, but that's not me."

"Damn, that's messed up. So what are you gonna do?"

"Nancy said that maybe he's going through a phase, but I don't think so. I wish she was right, though, because I miss him so much."

I closed my eyes. Dayshawn was trying to move up in the world and Shareeka was holding him back by continuing to live in the past. She'd better be careful. There are a lot of desperate women out there, and taking this man from her would be real, real easy.

Chapter 29

SAUNDRA

I'd somehow learned my new job and kept the bills paid over the last few weeks. God obviously had me cradled in His arms, because between all of that and spending my free time at the hospital, I should have collapsed by now. Daddy and I greeted each other with civility whenever we ran into each other. He made Yero laugh, and for that I was truly grateful. Someday soon, I'd have to tell him that.

Yero was undergoing chemotherapy. His hair was falling out in clumps and we finally decided to shave the rest of it off. Now his locks were gone. He looked into a hand mirror and cried. Turned away from me, pressed his face into a pillow, and cried.

A few weeks ago, I would have cried too, but now I was either numb or hardened.

It turned out that I wasn't a match for bone marrow, so the doctors were testing some members of his biological family real soon. That was the part that Yero found so terrifying. That and the fact that doctors and hospitals might take up much of his life for the next few years even if the disease went into remission.

Asha called yesterday, wanting to know if I needed anything. I swallowed my pride and told her that I needed money. Lots of it. As much as she could spare. She promised to get it for me, but there was a catch in her voice. I didn't know if she wanted to cry because she'd have to ask Nick for it or because she planned to delve into her treasured savings account. When I was staying at Asha's apartment two years ago, I came across her bank statement. Okay, I didn't come across it. I was going through her things. She had $120,000 in the account. Most of it came from her married lovers. So she owed that money to the wives and children whose lives were hurt by her selfishness. Since she couldn't give it to them, I'd take it without a qualm.

I'd do anything legal to get my beloved Yero up off that hospital bed and back home with me where he belonged.

Chapter 30

ED

My behavior for the next day and a half was very unprofessional. After my girlfriend dumped me (over a dinner I ended up paying for), I holed up in my one-bedroom apartment getting drunk on straight scotch and listening to Miles Davis. After that and the head-splitting hangover, I spent most of the next day sitting on the stoop of the apartment building, which was in Manhattan's Hell's Kitchen district, watching the tenants go in and out. I didn't check my phone messages during any of that time. When I did, there was only one. It was from *her*. She said that she understood how upset I was but she hoped we could remain friends. I threw the phone out of the window and watched it fly across the street and land in a vacant lot.

Then I went back to work.

Back at my desk, I made a lot of calls to set up interviews. Shareeka Ellison, Bruce Benedict, Eric Collins, and Nancy's mother and brother were all gracious. Vernon Mann and his wife, Ivie, were another story. He very rudely told me that to talk to him I'd need a subpoena. She just plain cursed me out and hung up.

I was in a mean and nasty mood. It made me put them both first on my list.

Vernon was coming out of the Time Warner Building on East

Fiftieth Street when I stopped him. He was a nondescript middle-aged executive, and for a moment I wondered what Nancy had seen in him. I walked right up on him and interrupted the conversation he was having with two white men.

"Hello, Vernon. My name is Ed Winsome, the private investigator who called you this morning. As I told you, I'm here to talk about your previous relationship with a woman named Nancy Rosa St. Bart. You do remember Nancy, don't you, Vernon? Maybe you can help her before she gets killed."

He opened and closed his mouth like a fish. The white boys looked uneasy, murmured something about catching up with him later, and practically jogged away from us.

"That was my fucking boss," he sputtered. "You goddamn idiot!"

I stood there in my blue jeans, T-shirt, and sneakers.

"Nancy almost ruined my life once. What the hell is she up to now?"

"You're going to need an alibi, Mr. Mann. You and your wife."

He was practically screaming now. "An alibi for what?"

"The early morning hours of April second . . . between three thirty and four a.m. That is when someone placed a bleeding dog whose throat had been freshly cut on her property."

He blanched. "Jesus!"

"When is the last time you talked to Nancy?"

"I'm calling the police!"

"Good. It'll save me the trouble."

He had pulled out his cell phone. Now he put it back. "Look, I'm sorry that I was rude to you on the phone, but I haven't talked to Nancy in a little over two years. Our story is not complicated. I had an affair. My wife found out. She and Nancy had words. Lots of words. I ended things with Nancy. I thought she had moved on with her life. Obviously, I was wrong. Why on earth does she think I'd get behind something like this?"

"Maybe you're screwing around again and Ivie thinks that Nancy is the woman you're seeing. Maybe Ivie did it to warn Nancy that she's not playing this time around."

He sneered. "If you were any good at your job, you'd know that I'm faithful to my wife these days. Now get out of my way."

Vernon reached out an arm to push me, but something in my eyes must have stopped him. "Please. I swear to you that I'm no threat to Nancy. Please. Leave us alone."

Chapter 31

SHAREEKA

It was a warm afternoon and Shareeka was enjoying a game of checkers with her son's girlfriend when the maid came into the family room holding a cardboard box.

"This was left at the gate for you, Mrs. Ellison. Don't you think it should have wrapping on it?"

Shareeka glanced at it. Her name and address were written in red pen on the top. "Maybe somebody is trying to get Dayshawn to listen to an audition tape or something. People get mighty creative when they want to get his attention."

Thelma held out a hand. "Let me see. I bet the music on it is totally wack."

The maid handed it over and left the room.

Thelma opened the lid and looked inside. She just stared without speaking until Shareeka started toward her.

"Thelma? Gurl, are you all right?"

Her voice seemed to reactivate the young girl, who promptly dropped the box like it was burning her hands.

A dead rat, cut in three pieces, fell onto Shareeka's carpet.

Thelma started screaming.

Shareeka swallowed hard and backed away from the disgusting mess. "Crenshaw! Crenshaw!"

The sound of her voice sounded like a needle screeching across the surface of an old record album.

Crenshaw came running with Cheery at his heels. The little girl froze, just looking at the floor as though staring would turn it into something pleasant like a new doll.

Crenshaw ushered the three females out of the room and into the foyer. He shook Thelma like a rag doll. "Baby! Stop! Stop!"

He took control of the situation. "Y'all go outside. There was a piece of red paper on the floor. I'm going to see what it is and call the police."

Shareeka grabbed Thelma and Cheery.

They ran outside and stood there. Unable to move or speak.

A muffled ringing came from inside the house and they could hear Crenshaw talking to someone.

Cheery moaned and hugged her mother around the waist.

This was the scene as Penelope's car came up the driveway. She jumped out, too angry to see that all was not right at the Ellison home. Her face was mottled with rage as she approached.

"Get in the car, Thelma. Right now! Get in the car and don't give me any lip. Mama said that Mrs. Dart saw Crenshaw in Rite-Aid yesterday at the checkout counter. He was buying condoms, Thelma. Condoms!"

Crenshaw came out at that exact moment, but he was too upset to even notice that Penelope was there. "Mama, I got something to tell you."

"And I got something to tell you," Penelope screamed. "You better not lay a finger on my daughter. Do you hear me?"

Shareeka whirled around and stuck her face straight up in Penelope's. "Shut the fuck up!"

Crenshaw looked from one to the other.

"What do you have to tell me?" Shareeka asked impatiently.

"I don't want to say it in front of Cheery."

"Whisper."

He whispered in his mother's ear and her eyes became huge.

"Call Nancy and tell her to get out of that house. Then call the police."

It finally occurred to Penelope that something out of the ordinary was taking place. "What is going on here?"

"A box came for Mommy. A dead rat was inside," Cheery said miserably. "Thelma started screaming."

Penelope reached out for her only child. "Honey, are you all right?"

Thelma leaned on her shoulder. "Yes."

"Who would do such a thing?"

Shareeka pulled Penelope to the side and told her about Nancy's situation. "Crenshaw said there is a note on red paper that says I better stay away from Nancy or somebody is going to kill my kids."

Chapter 32

ED

Ivie Mann's husband had clearly called ahead and warned his wife that I would act a fool in front of her coworkers if she didn't cooperate. She was an executive at an insurance firm down in the Chelsea area of Manhattan. Her secretary, a pretty young thing who said her name was Suriana, came out to greet me. On the way down a long, gray-carpeted hallway, she asked after my health, offered me coffee, water, and a pastry. I was expecting a coupon good for a back rub at my favorite spa when she stopped and held out one arm like a game show mannequin.

"May I present Ivie Mann."

Ivie was alarmingly thin and had no charisma. She was pale enough to pass for white if she chose and had short brown hair chopped up so that one side was longer than the other. Her lack of charisma at all, and that made her ugly. I accepted her offer of a seat and promised not to take up much of her time.

"Can you tell me about your relationship with Nancy Rosa St. Bart?"

"We never met."

"But you did speak a few times on the phone, correct?"

"Yes. I found out that she was having an affair with my husband and made it clear that I wouldn't tolerate it."

"She says that you threatened to kill her."

Ivie just stared at me and said nothing. I didn't blame her. What she had done was illegal.

"She says that you called her several times. That is harassment."

Another stare.

"Mrs. Mann, I'm a private investigator who has been hired by Ms. St. Bart, but I used to be a cop. I still have friends on the force. Please help me or I'll have to ask them to persuade you to be cooperative."

"You haven't asked me any question that I can answer."

"Have you called Nancy's home in the past twelve months?"

"No."

"Have you been in the town of Hercsville, Long Island, in the past twelve months?"

"Do you know anyone who wants to harm Nancy?"

We both chuckled at that one.

"Why did you harass Nancy and then stay with your husband?"

"What does that mean?"

"I've always wondered why a woman attacks the other woman instead of the man who promised, usually in a church before God, to be faithful to her."

Her face turned red. "We went to counseling and worked it out."

"As far as you know, has he committed adultery since his affair with Nancy ended?"

She hesitated long enough for me to know that he was jumping in and out of beds all over town.

There was nothing else to learn. I left.

Nancy had given me her mother's address out in Brooklyn. I knew that part of Bedford Stuyvesant well. There was never any place to park, so I took the subway. According to Nancy, her brother, Randall, lived with their mother, whose first name was Kate. That is, when Randall wasn't doing time for armed robbery.

The building was far too nice for an elderly woman living on a fixed income to afford, so I gave Nancy props for taking care of Mama. They lived on the sixteenth floor of a doorman, elevator building. The doorman wasn't wearing gloves and a uniform with a braid on the shoulder, but he carried himself like he was. After a murmured phone conversation with the occupants of apartment 4E, he smiled and gestured behind him.

"Walk straight through the lobby and turn left at the mirrored wall. The elevator bank is right there."

I thanked him and moved silently through the squeaky clean space.

A man answered the door when I knocked. He stood around five eight, which was the same height as Nancy. His head was bald. His face was round and so were his features. There was no hair on his face. He looked like a cherub. I almost laughed.

"I'm Randall St. Bart."

"Thanks for letting me up, man. I'm Ed Winsome."

We shook hands. He stood back and held the door open.

I was standing in a small living room that had tangerine carpet on the floor, a tangerine pullout sofa against the long wall, and a blue recliner on the short wall. In between were wooden tables. There were no pictures on the wall. Everything was clean, but the place smelled like cigar smoke.

He gestured toward the sofa. "Please. Have a seat."

I expected him to take the recliner, but instead he sat a few inches away, hunching forward so that he could see my eyes.

"Mama isn't here. She is at her sister's house in Staten Island."

Nancy hadn't mentioned any other relatives.

"I know you're here about Nancy."

"Yes. Did she tell you the story?"

He shrugged. "Yes, she called and filled me in. But it doesn't matter. Even if she hadn't, I'd still know. Nobody comes here about me unless it's the cops."

"Sorry to hear that, man."

Another shrug. "It's cool. It's not like they're picking on me or anything. How can I help you?"

"Does your sister have any enemies?"

"I would guess that my sister has nothing but enemies."

"Why is that?"

"Because she goes around fucking with people without meaning to."

"Example?"

"Well, one time this dude broke up with her. Nancy does not handle rejection well, but Dude didn't know that." Randall laughed. It was the hoarse sound of a longtime smoker. "I bet his ass found out."

"What did she do?"

"Told his parole officer that he threatened her. Cops picked his ass up and threw him back in jail."

"That doesn't sound like someone who doesn't mean to cause harm."

Randall waved his hands impatiently. "She didn't want him back in jail, man. She just wanted a shoulder to cry on and his parole officer showed up at the wrong time."

"Well, did the guy threaten her or not?"

"He threatened to kick her ass if she didn't stop calling his new girlfriend. It's just something he said because he didn't know what else to do. He wasn't really going to hit her. Nancy just figured that the PO would tell his client to work things out with her before something bad happened. There is no way Nancy would have said anything if she thought he was going back to jail. She's not evil or mean. Just can't control her emotions and does stupid shit sometimes."

"Do you think this guy is trying to get back at her by scaring her?"

"Nah. All that shit happened when Nancy was about nineteen years old. Why would he wait so long?"

"What happened to him?"

"Last I heard, he married that same woman and they have a little kid."

So Nancy was capable of ruining lives when she didn't get her way. Interesting. Obviously, I needed her to make up another list. Something like Dumb Shit That Hurt Others.

"What else, man? I got an appointment."

"Are you younger than Nancy?"

"Yeah, I'm thirty-seven. She's thirty-nine."

"Any other brothers and sisters?"

"Not by my mama. Who knows about Pops? That muthafucka probl'y got kids all over the world."

"Where is he now?"

"Dead. Enough about him. Move on."

"Do you love your sister?"

His eyes told me that he loved Nancy more than anyone else in the world.

He seemed shocked by the question. "Yes. I'd do anything for her."

I wondered if he'd kill a dog to help her get publicity and a new acting gig.

"Are the two of you close?"

He sighed and rubbed his forehead. "We used to be when we were kids. Not anymore. Shit happens, man. You got kids, man?"

"No," I answered ruefully. "Never had a wife. Never had babies."

He reared back. "You straight?"

"Yeah, man. What the fuck? A brother gotta be gay just because he's single?"

"My bad. I like you, man. Where you from?"

"Indianapolis. I couldn't wait to get out of there. Came to New York after college and became a cop."

"No shit? I knew you were a cop by the way you knocked on the door."

I studied him closely. "Nancy told me you did some time."

"Time, time, and mo time," he chuckled.

The caller was right. He was a dumb ass. But why was Nancy's mother a coward?

"You gonna go straight from now on?"

"Probably not," he answered frankly. "But I'm not getting myself sent away till you find whoever is fucking with my sister. You might need a different kind of help, and I've got to be on the street for that."

I knew that he was offering me access to people who would maim, stalk, or kill on command. I didn't judge him. He knew bad people. Someone very bad had left blood on his sister's doorstep.

"Randall, can I ask you something?"

"What?"

"How come there are no pictures on these bare-ass white walls?"

"Peep this. It is some psychological shit that Mama and Nancy don't think I'm hip to. It works this way. Nancy was always winning stuff. Then she became an actress and got her name and pictures in the papers and magazines. They think that if Mama puts all that stuff up on the walls, it will make me more depressed and I'll never get my life together. So we all pretend that ain't shit ever happened in our family worth putting on the walls."

How sad.

"Sounds like they love you."

"Yeah."

There was silence.

"Have you ever been to your sister's house?"

"The place she lives at now? Nah. Mama never been there either. Nancy always has some excuse why we can't come."

I made a mental note to ask Nancy why she kept her family at arm's length.

"So you haven't seen the Denzel Washington wallpaper?"

He looked puzzled. "What you talkin' 'bout, man?"

"It's not real wallpaper. Just floor-to-ceiling pictures of Denzel Washington in every single room. Even the kitchen and bathroom. Any idea why she would do that?"

"You scaring me, man. Sounds like she's buggin' the fuck out. What's the address out there?"

I stood up and stretched. "You can't get in without Nancy's permission. They've got a real strict security system. A man in a booth with a gun writes down the license plate number of every car that comes through. Plus he calls the house to get permission to lift the gate."

Randall grinned. "I could get in there if I wanted to."

I believed him. "Remember that I might need you out here on the street."

"Yeah. Yeah, you're right. But doesn't that make your job easier?"

"How?"

"Whoever left that dog on the step must live in that town. Right?"

"Right. Or know someone who does."

Chapter 33

ED

Randall and I rode the elevator down to the street. Then he went off to his appointment and I found a Jamaican restaurant where I could kill some time until his mother got home. With a plate of peas and rice in front of me, I checked out the atmosphere and revised my opinion of the woman I was trying to protect. I used a paper napkin to make a list of my discoveries:

1. She was emotionally unstable.
2. She had little control over her emotions.
3. She could not handle rejection.
4. She had an agent who was concerned about her.
5. She had very little money.
6. She had a brother who adored her.

It wasn't much. Just enough for me to realize that Nancy had wounded someone and either did not realize it at the time or didn't give any weight to her crime. She thought like a child. Since she wasn't hurting any longer, the other person shouldn't be either. Life doesn't work that way, but since no one had taught her that, the lists she had made for me would be useless.

The restaurant was called The Hot Pot. There were more workers than customers in the place, but the food was delicious. The space was tiny—about eight tables covered with plaid table-cloths—but clean. The staff chattered and laughed among themselves—their lyrical accents rising and falling with the clinking of dishes and silverware.

I wondered why Nancy and her brother looked so totally unalike. Did they have the same father? Maybe the mother would let me borrow some photo albums and yearbooks. I wasn't interested in seeing Nancy's childhood photos, but I did need to jog her memory of old, disgruntled friends.

A young woman walked past my table two or three times before I got the hint. The sister was flirting with me. She was far too young, no older than twenty-five—but very pretty. I answered her smile with an invitation.

"Would you join me for a cup of coffee?"

She glanced toward the kitchen. "I can't. I go to work in five minutes."

"What is your name, gorgeous?"

She blushed. "Meseleen."

"Very pretty. Are you a student?"

Meseleen eased herself into the empty chair at my little table. "Oh, sir. I want so much to go to school in this country. I want get a CPA . . . you understand?"

I understood perfectly. She needed a sponsor and would probably offer me money and whatever else I wanted in exchange for a green card.

"That's wonderful, Meseleen. I wish you all the luck in the world. Could you ask someone to get my check, please?"

Her slim face registered her disappointment, but she handled the situation with grace. With a slight nod of her head, she did as I asked. As she walked away, her slim hips worked the hell out of a flouncy yellow skirt.

Nancy's mother gave me a warm greeting and ushered me into her home. The daughter was the spitting image of her mother. I explained that I'd already been inside to speak with Randall. There was music playing softly on an old-fashioned stereo. An old tune by Smokey Robinson.

I accepted her offer of tea and pound cake. We made small talk about taxes, the weather, and the rising cost of everything before I got to the point.

"Someone has been threatening Nancy and it is important that we find out who it is."

She was wearing a blue vest, matching pants, and a pair of red sandals. She fiddled with the gold buttons on the vest.

"Bubbee mentioned that."

"Who is Bubbee?"

"Sorry. It's Nancy's nickname. Everyone in the family calls her that."

Randall didn't, but I kept my mouth shut.

"The situation is getting worse."

She looked frightened. "Did the woman call again?"

No one had told her about the dog with the picture in its mouth. Maybe she had a heart condition.

"Yes."

"Jesus!"

"It's pretty bad," I agreed. "Can you think of anyone who might want to hurt her?"

"I don't know anyone in Nancy's life except Bruce."

"What about him?"

She snorted. "Bubbee should be the one hurting him. He has free room, board, food, clothes, and he drives the car she worked so hard to buy. What kind of man is that? Why, he ain't no better than Randall, and Bubbee is always complaining about my son livin' off me."

I agreed with her a hundred percent.

"Well," I said softly, "Bruce is a struggling comedian. Nancy understands that."

"Puh-leeze. He ain't twenty years old. Do you know that he used to work in a bank? That man wasn't thinkin' 'bout no show business till he met Bubbee. He saw a lonely woman with money and jumped on the gravy train."

Nancy and the vicious caller had referred to this woman as a coward. Why?

I took a deep breath and plunged in. "Did Nancy tell you that her caller referred to you as a coward and Randall, a dumb-ass?"

Her eyes flashed. "Yes, she did. I don't understand why. Anybody who has ever met me knows that I'm not scared of nothin' or nobody and Randall is just troubled. Do you know that he once read through a whole set of encyclopedias? He is not dumb."

"I agree with you."

She relaxed a little. "Both my kids finished high school and Nancy has two years of college."

"What did Nancy do between high school and her work on *The Bridesmaid?*"

Her face brightened. "She got lots of bit roles on TV and in the movies. When there was no paying work, she took to the road doing summer stock. Anything that gave her a chance to get on a stage and act."

"Are the two of you close?"

"She sighed. "Bubbee pretends that we are, but I know the truth."

"That's an interesting answer. Could you tell me more?"

"No. What does all this have to do with those phone calls?"

"Maybe nothing," I admitted. "But I was a cop for many years. Sometimes the answers to these puzzles come out of left field."

"We're not close but I keep hoping that that will change."

"Good enough," I said.

"I hear she got a nice house," she replies.

"Bruce. He comes with her to see me sometime."

She said the name "Bruce" like it was the word *leprosy*.

"Does Nancy know how you feel about Bruce?"

"You damn right. What kind of mother would I be if I didn't say something?"

"I understand, but when people are in love, they don't want to hear it."

"Love?"

"Don't you think she loves him?"

"Not the way you mean. She loves having a companion, that's all."

"Do you have any pictures or yearbooks I can borrow? I'd like to walk Nancy through the past ten years and see if anything jogs her memory."

"Mr. Winsome, if there are pictures of Nancy's life during that time period, you'll have to get them from her. My stuff is way older. Would you like to see them?"

"Sure, but can I ask you a question first?"

"Shoot."

"When did she start talking about Denzel Washington?"

"The actor? Never. Why do you ask? Is he mixed up in this? Has she ever met him?"

"I'm not sure."

"Then why did you ask?"

"Because she has hundreds of his pictures in her house."

"When she was a little girl, I used to clip out every picture of Sam Cooke that I could find and put them in a scrapbook. Nancy liked to put the glue on the back before I pasted them in. What can I say? It was lonely with just me and the kids."

"Where was their father?"

"Living with another woman."

"I'm sorry."

"So was I."

"Randall tells me that he died."

"I told Randy that he is probably dead. He used to call me once in a while. The calls stopped about four years ago."

"Did he call Nancy?"

Her entire demeanor changed. She suddenly became cold. Her body was rigid. "Look, I'm tired. Do you want to see the pictures or not?"

My cell phone rang before I could answer. It was my client.

"Hi, Nancy!"

"Shareeka got a dead rat in the mail. Please meet me at her house right now!"

"Nancy, calm down and tell me what happened."

"Somebody said she better stop being friends with me or Cheery and Crenshaw are gonna get killed."

"I'm on my way!"

I flipped the phone shut.

Nancy's mother was wringing her hands. Her face was taut with fear. "I'm going with you."

Chapter 34

SAUNDRA

Asha was treating me to the performance of an off-off-Broadway play so I was oiling my locks and listening to her talk about Dayshawn and the marvelous career as a film producer, which would be hers in the future. That's what I like about Asha. No matter how far down in the dumps she gets, the spring back is always fascinating. It was her idea for us to go out tonight and, I knew that she just wanted to take my mind off Yero. It was very thoughtful of her.

The play we were going to see was called *The Proper Job at the Proper Time.* It's a mystery about a woman accused of killing her boss in order to get a promotion. Asha even took me shopping for a new outfit to wear tonight. I chose a knee-length, off-the-shoulder white dress with matching sandals. She paid eight hundred dollars for a dress by some designer whose name I can't even pronounce and a pair of silver, strappy sandals.

Yero thought that I should get out more and I didn't need to come to the hospital every day. That's crazy. If it were me lying on my back, I'd expect to see his face every day.

Asha was using a curling iron on her hair. She was sitting at my kitchen table and working on it, strand by strand. "When I first called Dayshawn, I was real nervous. But he answered the phone and just started talking like we were old friends. He is going to start filming a movie real soon and he says that he'll use me but I won't have to do stuff for everybody else. Just for him."

"So how does Nick feel about this?"

"He's happy as a duck in water. In fact, his mother told me that he's been bragging about all the famous people he's gonna meet when I become a big-time producer."

I laughed. "You and Nick are both starstruck."

"You know what?"

"What?"

"I have a feeling that Dayshawn is going to hit on me."

My voice rose. "And of course you'll turn him down, seeing as the two of you are both married and his wife got you the job."

"I meant that we'll probably sleep together a couple of times during the filming. I didn't say that we were leaving our spouses or getting Shareeka all upset."

"I'm surprised that you are able to sleep at night. That is some real scandalous shit that you just said."

"I've been reading up on the entertainment business, Saundra. This kind of thing goes on all the time. But when the movie wraps, the affair ends."

She turned and smiled at me. "Remember what happened between Sanaa Lathan and Denzel Washington while they were filming *Out of Time?*"

"They've both said that those rumors are completely untrue."

"What are they supposed to say? Yes, we screwed each other's brains out and we hope that Pauletta isn't mad? Grow up, Saundra."

"Fine, Asha. Go on and fuck Bustacap. Just don't give me the whole entertainment business shit. You've been sleeping with other women's husbands for years. You'd do it if he was a damn veterinarian. So cut the crap!"

Asha had nothing to say to that. Meaning that she knew I was right and wanted to drop the subject. I wasn't letting her go that easy.

"What is the name of the movie?" I asked.

"What movie are you talking about?" Asha answered.

"The movie that you and Busta are going to screw your way through."

She put the curler down and flipped her hair around. "I don't know what it's called but it's about this guy. He's like a truck driver or something. He agrees to take this woman's kids across the country to see their father. The kids end up seeing him as a daddy figure and the woman falls in love with him. At the end of the film, they are a family. Dayshawn plays the truck driver."

I had to admit that working on a movie set sounded like fun. If anyone could network and build a new career out of this one opportunity, it was most definitely Asha.

"Who is playing his love interest?"

"I don't know yet. He tried to get Theresa Tanner, but she doesn't respect him as a filmmaker. That is a big problem for Dayshawn. Because he used to be a rapper, the black folk in the film business look down on him. They all had to train and work so hard to get where they are, it pisses them off that he just up one day and decided to do this."

"Is it a movie with rap music in it?"

"No."

"Then Theresa should just go on and do it. It's a paycheck. She hasn't been in any movies that I've seen for the past three years."

"Dayshawn says that she graduated from the Yale School of Drama, which is like a big deal. She made her acting debut in a small part on Broadway. It all sounds like a bunch of snooty bullshit if you ask me."

My hair was done. All I had to do was lotion up and slide into the dress. "Well, if there was any justice, Theresa Tanner would have an Oscar by now. She is so, so talented."

"We've got to hurry up, Saundra."

"Are you finished with your hair?"

She looked this way and that in the mirror. "I'm not sure. How does it look?"

"You look like a beauty queen."

My doorbell rang. I pressed the intercom.

"Who is it?"

"Khari."

Khari was Yero's younger brother. What was he doing here? Maybe Yero needed something and Khari dropped by to get it on the way to the hospital.

I buzzed him into the building and stood waiting with my front door open. When he came into view, I could tell he'd been crying. He pulled me into his arms and held me tight.

"Saundra, I'm so, so sorry. Yero had a heart attack."

I couldn't breathe. My chest felt compressed. My head hurt. "When?"

"A little while ago. I was visiting him when it happened."

Behind me, Asha started to cry.

"Is he all right?"

Khari let me go and started pounding on the wall. The tears ran down his face. "He died, Saundra. Yero's gone!"

Chapter 35

ED

By the time Kate and I took a cab to get my car, loaded the albums and yearbooks in the trunk, and then crawled through bumper-to-bumper traffic to reach Long Island, it was more than an hour and a half from the time Nancy called until we pulled up to Shareeka's house. There was a uniformed cop stationed outside. He called the woman of the house outside to verify who we were.

Shareeka Ellison may have been frightened and hysterical when she called Nancy, but by the time I met her, she was just plain furious. She was a beautiful woman with big, luscious brown eyes and pouty lips. I could have done without the long blond weave, but she carried it with style and confidence. She was wearing white stirrup pants, matching sandals, and some type of white, gauzy top. I could see straight through it to her white bra.

Nancy had told her about me, she said.

The officer stepped aside and we followed her in. She never stopped talking.

"I can't even believe this muthafuckin' shit. Nancy can put up with this psycho bitch if she wants to, but I'm not about to have it. I called Dayshawn, but he ain't answering his cell. We gonna get some serious security up in this place, and if that don't work, I'll find the bitch myself and blow her goddamned brains out."

By this time we were in the living room. I was astonished to see a huge fountain in the middle of the room. This wasn't Rome! It even had running water. Nancy, Bruce, and a woman I didn't recognize were just sitting around on the longest and most circular sofa that I had ever seen.

Nancy was staring at the television, but her mind was somewhere else. I shook her shoulder and she looked up.

"Ed! Mama! What are you doing here?"

"You called, remember?"

"I meant what is Mama doing here?"

"Bubbee, are you all right?"

Nancy stood up and they hugged and kissed. There appeared to be genuine warmth between them. I remember that Kate said her daughter pretended that they were close. She certainly did. But, then again, Nancy was an actress.

Nancy gestured toward the unknown woman. "Ed, Mama, this is Penelope Brewster."

Penelope Brewster nodded her head slightly in recognition.

"Ed is a private detective," Nancy said to no one in particular.

"Why don't you fill me in? Exactly what happened here today?"

Nancy didn't have a chance to tell the story. My question opened the floor back up for Shareeka. She told me everything and then ended with "The bitch ain't even got no heart. I mean, this is some cowardly, punk-ass shit. If she got a problem with Nancy, she need to just step to her and settle it. Like a woman."

"There were a lot of police here," Nancy told me. "They wrote everything down, took the rat, and left."

"I planned to visit the local precinct today anyway," I told her. "I need to see their photos and whatever else they're willing to share with me."

"I can't believe that all of this has been going on. Crenshaw never said a word and neither did Thelma."

Shareeka gave Penelope an angry stare. "I didn't tell them what was going on with Nancy."

"I understand that to a point, but you could have informed me. After all, Thelma spends a lot of time in this house. If she was in danger, I had a right to know."

While the two women quibbled, I sat back and watched Bruce. I know how it feels to be tired of a relationship. To know that whatever you once felt for the woman does not exist anymore. To want out but not know how to end it. Bruce was there. I didn't think it had anything to do with what was going on. He had been in his current state for quite some time. I wondered if Denzel had been the wallpaper when he moved in. If so, he was a fool. He caught me looking at him and turned away. I sympathized with the brother. He was wishing he'd split before Nancy's drama started. Now it would look real fucked-up if he dumped her.

"Where are your children?" I asked Shareeka.

"Upstairs."

Penelope chimed in. "My daughter is there too, but we're about to leave."

Shareeka sneered. "Her daughter goes with my son, Crenshaw. But the good doctor here don't like that much."

"Doctor?"

She stood up and grabbed her handbag. "I'm a clinical psychologist."

"Up until today, my son was one of her patients."

Penelope stopped moving. "What is that supposed to mean?"

"It means, Dr. Penny, that Crenshaw ain't comin' back."

Penelope sighed. "You're probably right. He needs to see someone who isn't involved in his personal life."

"Do you have a card?" I asked. "I'd like to talk to you at some point."

She gave it to me and headed upstairs to collect her daughter.

Chapter 36

ASHA

Yero's funeral was packed with mourners. He had been a good son, a great brother, and a wonderful husband. Everyone from the Queens neighborhood he'd grown up in was there.

The services were held at Canaan Baptist Church on 116th Street. Even though he had not been a member, his mother had served the church faithfully for more than forty years. His family was devastated and I knew that their cries, mingled with those of my sister, would ring on and off in my head for years to come.

The front pew was crowded with family members who sat on either side of his mother and Saundra, and the next five rows held other relatives. Nick and I were not close enough to give Saundra any comforting pats, but the pastor's sermon could be heard clearly since he was using a microphone.

I tried to concentrate on the pastor's biblical quotations and the eulogy, but my eyes couldn't turn away from the bronze coffin covered with flowers. Saundra had decided to keep it closed because Yero's suffering showed on his face. For a while, I prayed as she cried. Prayed that Yero, even though he wasn't a man known for practical jokes, would suddenly open the lid of the coffin and smile that lazy grin of his. Prayed that my sister would find the strength to go on without her soul mate. Prayed that his poor mama would smile again someday.

It just couldn't be true that Yero wouldn't ever have the three kids he'd always talked about or mix up any more veggie pizzas. It wasn't fair! There were crack dealers, child abusers, woman beaters, and other scum walking the streets right now, healthy as you please. They were no good to anyone, not even themselves.

I didn't realize that Saundra was crying aloud until Khari gathered her into his arms. His chest was heaving with sobs, but he hugged her tight. "Be strong, baby. Yero is in a better place."

Why did people always say that? Yero's better place was with Saundra, sitting patiently while she oiled his locks.

Several of Yero's friends from the post office got up and expressed their sorrow. A woman, probably the church secretary, read the cards and letters that had come in and then the choir started singing.

That was the worst of all. I knew that Saundra needed me when those voices started soaring so high that they seemed to touch the ceiling.

"I've got to get to my sister," I whispered.

Nick understood and helped me get past all the other people who were sitting in our row. He kept a firm grip on my elbow as I wobbled down the aisle. By this time, Saundra's head was in her mother-in-law's lap and she was clearly hysterical.

I whispered in her ear, but she was beyond hearing me. Nick and I didn't know what to do. Just as I was beginning to panic, a woman dressed completely in white approached us and gestured for Nick and me to stand back.

At first, I didn't move but then I realized that she was a deaconess. She held something under Saundra's nose, and her head rose. She looked at me and held her arms out. Several people scooted over to make room for me.

I didn't let go of my sister until the service was over. After the burial, she'd be coming home with me.

It was better for her to live with us until she figured out what to do next. If I had my way, she'd never see the apartment where she and her husband had been so happy, ever again.

Chapter 37

NANCY

It was the day before Nancy and Eric were due to meet with the Fab Floor Shine people and she was reclining in a hammock out in her backyard. The midday sun toasted her bikini-clad body. Sunglasses protected her eyes. She swung back and forth wondering if she should take Dr. Penny up on her offer. Now that she was no longer treating Crenshaw, the doctor had offered her a couple of psychotherapy sessions to ease her through this stressful time. It was a good idea but Nancy had tried therapy several times before and had always stopped going for the same reason: They wanted to talk about her parents. Even if she gave them all the dirt right up front: Yes, I was a sexually abused child. No, my mother did not know anything about it and even when she found out did not blow the muthafucka's brains out like she should have. Now let's move on and talk about the problems I'm having in my career and relationships. Even if she gave them a speech just like that, the doctors would still want to "explore" the sexual abuse issue. They would press and press until one day she just would fail to show up for her appointment. Then they would call and call to "check up on her" until she said something nasty to push them away for good.

Dr. Penny seemed like a real nice lady, a little on the uptight and conservative side, but competent. It would be nice to have someone to talk to about all the misery in her life, but she had been through the whole spiel too many times.

What would happen if she didn't tell Dr. Penny the dirt? She'd tried that one too. All therapists want to know about your parents. There had been times when she'd simply refused to discuss them at all. In that case, the doctor would spend most of his energy trying to trick her into mentioning something, anything, that would open a window into her past. It usually went something like this:

Doctor: So how was the banquet last night?

Nancy: Fabulous. I did work on the issues we've been talking about.

Doctor: How?

Nancy: I didn't skip the cocktail hour out of fear of the small talk.

Doctor: Good.

Nancy: And I tried not to ramble on and on, monopolizing the conversation when someone spoke to me.

Doctor: Very good.

Nancy: Thanks.

Doctor: Do cocktail parties remind you of birthday parties when you were a kid?

Nancy: No.

Doctor: Is that because you didn't have any childhood birthday parties or because you don't want to tell me about them?

Nancy: My mother would have the neighborhood children over for ice cream and cake.

Doctor: Did your mother like to bake?

Nancy: I see where this is going. Didn't I tell you that I didn't want to discuss my parents? Didn't you hear me say that?

Doctor: Nancy, you're becoming agitated.

Nancy: I was perfectly calm when I came in here. If you ever mention them again, I'm not coming back. I swear it.

Weeks, sometimes months would go by and everything would be all right. But, sooner or later, the therapist would bring up the subject again. Then it was over.

Why put Dr. Penny through that?

Nancy sighed. It was nice of Mama to come all the way out to Long Island to check on her. Really nice. Mama was a good woman who certainly loved her children. She was just fucked-up in the head. How could she ever speak to Dad again after what he had done? When Randall told her that he had been calling the house up until four years ago, Nancy couldn't believe it. She had been too scared to have it out with Mama. It would simply lead to a screaming match. She would end up crying in frustration. Mama would fall back on her same old crutch. "I did everything for y'all. All I get back is complaints and insults. Why do you even bother with me? I mean, if I hated somebody, I'd just stay the fuck away from them."

How did you answer that?

If things got even more heated, Mama would say, "Don't worry. I won't live forever. One of these days, you'll wish you could hear my voice."

Mama lying dead?

It was too horrible to think about.

No, it was best to say nothing about the phone calls, but she did wonder what on earth there was left for her parents to talk about. Did they just avoid the subject of Nancy? They had to. Right?

Bruce came out of the house. She watched as he shuffled toward the hammock. Finally, he reached her.

"I've got to talk to you, Nancy."

"So talk."

He put his hand on the hammock to stop it from rocking. "Remember, a few weeks ago I told you that we needed to talk?"

"Yes."

"Do you remember that it was before you told me about the phone calls and before the dead dog was found?"

"Yes. Why?"

"Because I don't want you to think that what I'm about to say has anything to do with what you're going through."

"Bruce," she murmured. "What is it?"

He shifted awkwardly from one foot to the other. "I'm moving out of your house, Nancy."

Nancy sat up so abruptly that he had to keep her from falling out of the hammock. "Why? Where will you live?"

"In Milwaukee."

"Milwaukee?"

"Yeah. There are a lot of comedy clubs and dinner theaters in that section of the country."

Nancy could smell the bullshit. "Are you breaking up with me, Bruce?"

"We can stay friends, but, uh . . ." His voice trailed off and he looked up at the sky, squinting against the sun.

"So when are you leaving?" Nancy's voice cracked and she hated herself for showing him how much it hurt.

"Tonight."

"How long have you been planning this, Bruce?"

"Does it matter?"

What a glib and neat answer. In other words, *I'm moving and I don't feel like having a conversation about all the details.* Was she just supposed to accept that? A burning heat started at her toes, worked its way to her ankles, then the legs. By the time it reached her stomach, she was out of the hammock. Her shades were off. Her chest was heaving. She was slapping Bruce in the face.

"Get out! Get the fuck out now! I mean it! Get all your raggedy-ass belongings out of my house right this minute!"

"Nancy," he pleaded. "Don't end it like this. Come on, we had some good times."

"I don't want to hear it!"

He grabbed her by the wrist to protect his face from any more blows. When she stopped struggling, he let go and walked back inside the house. His head was down.

Nancy sat down in the grass. She wrapped her arms around her chest and started to hum, rocking back and forth.

"I saw your picture in Essence. You look good."

She had recognized the voice. It came from way back. From acting workshops in Los Angeles? From her days running from one agent's office to the other, seeking representation? She had been pretty nasty to some of the receptionists.

"*We can stay friends.*"

She had been so good to Bruce. Why did people feel that hurting her was okay?

If she washed her hands thirty-two times instead of the usual sixteen times, maybe some of the hurt would flow down the drain along with the soap residue.

She jumped up, ran into the first-floor bathroom, and gripped the edge of the sink until her body stopped shaking. She washed her hands sixteen times with Ivory soap, then sixteen times with Zest. Then she rinsed them twenty-five times with warm water, followed by twenty-five times with cold water.

"*Don't worry, baby. I still love you.*"

It was a man's voice. Where did it come from? She stopped. Her hands were hanging in the air, dripping wet. She cocked her head to the side and listened.

"*Let Uriah Heep pack his things and go.*"

Nancy spotted him. It was the Denzel who hung fourth from the left, above the light switch on the right side of her bathroom wall. This Denzel was wearing a blue open-necked shirt. His lips were moving.

She clapped her wet hands in delight. He was right. Bruce was just like the character in *David Copperfield* by Charles Dickens. Uriah Heep bowed, scraped, smiled, and pretended to be grateful for charity. All the time he was a scheming, manipulative little shit.

She waited to see if the Denzel who hung fourth from the left would say anything else, but he just sat there, smiling.

When she stalked into the bedroom, Bruce was packing his belongings into two large trunks.

"You ain't gone yet?" she snarled.

Bruce snarled back, "I'll be out of here in fifteen minutes. I already called the cab."

"Good. Because Fourth from the left just told me that you're a Uriah Heep."

He stopped and stared at her like she'd grown two heads. "What did you just say?"

"You heard me. I know the truth now."

"Who is Fourth from the left?"

"None of your business. Just get out."

He threw a roll of socks into the trunk. "You need help, Nancy. Real bad. I hope that you get it, I really do."

"Fuck the banalities. If you're not out of here when I get back, I'm calling the cops."

She went back to the downstairs bathroom and told the Denzel who hung fourth from the left that she was grateful for his assessment of Bruce. "I should have seen it long ago, but I was just so lonely in this big house all by myself. Do you know what I'm going to do for you? I'm so grateful that you opened my eyes that I'm going to buy you a blue frame. Blue is the best color in the world."

His gorgeous lips moved. *"Thank you, Nancy. I'll be there soon. Will you come to see me?"*

Nancy thought for a moment. Denzel Washington was casting his new film somewhere in Manhattan. Her agent, Eric Collins, had mentioned that. She'd have to call and get the details. "Yes, I'll be there, baby. You can count on it."

Chapter 38

SHAREEKA

A week had passed since the rat was delivered to her door. Day-shawn had held her as she cried on his shoulder. He had also ordered a security system that took a picture of everyone who came to their front door. If that weren't enough, he now had an armed security guard roaming their property twenty-four hours a day.

Nevertheless, Shareeka wanted to take the whole nasty affair out of the closet and warn other potential victims before the sicko struck again.

She pulled up in front of a gray clapboard one-story building on Break Street. The bell jangled when she opened the front door and Janice Webster looked up with a smile. She worked alone, surrounded by rows of filing cabinets.

"Hello, Mrs. Ellison."

Shareeka sank down in the chair without being asked. "Hi. Whew! It is some hot out there today, isn't it?"

Janice nodded in agreement. "Yes, it is. I hope the air-conditioning in here isn't up too high. Is it?"

"Naw, I'm fine."

"So how can I help you, dear?"

"Did Penelope tell you about the rat that was delivered to my house?"

"Yes. In fact, she has told me everything she knows about that poor, unfortunate woman. Nancy is her name, right?"

"Yes. I'm here because I want you to run a story about the whole affair. I want everyone in Hercsville to know what has happened to me and Nancy."

Janice's eyes gleamed. "Are you sure? I figured that because of your husband's celebrity—"

Shareeka cut her off. "Later for that. I want a two-page spread in the *Hercsville Democrat* about it. I think that the villain is somewhere in this town. In the meantime, Ed has Nancy sitting around writing lists and shit. Maybe someone will read the story and remember seeing something strange. You never know."

"I agree. Who is Ed?"

"The private detective that Nancy has hired to find out who is behind this mess. As far as I'm concerned, he isn't doing a very good job."

"How is poor Nancy?" Janice murmured.

"I spoke to her this morning. Do you know what she did?"

"What?"

"Blew off the Fab Floor Shine people."

"I'm not following you."

Shareeka leaned forward so that both her arms were resting on the desk. "Nancy got written out of the soap opera she was working on. Her agent was getting her hooked up with the company that makes Fab Floor Shine. They were going to pay her crazy money to be their spokesperson. When I spoke with her this morning, she told me that she canceled the whole thing. Turned them down without even meeting with them."

Janice frowned. "She shouldn't be making major decisions at a time like this. She is probably frightened out of her mind and can't even think of working."

Shareeka hadn't thought of that. "You're right. I shouldn't have been so hard on her about it."

"Good. Now tell me your story and let's get it in print as soon as possible."

Shareeka talked for a whole hour. When the interview was over, she felt better. Cleansed. Ready to put the whole mess aside and go back to planning her party.

Chapter 39

SAUNDRA

I was sleeping in a spare room at Asha's house. I say sleeping instead of living because I hadn't given up the apartment that I shared with Yero. I couldn't do that yet. I just couldn't.

Every morning, I got up and took a cab to the Long Island Railroad and into Manhattan to work. My new job would be exciting if I wasn't so depressed. I went to the photography studios, got to know the stylists and models, and watched the shoots. Every night, I came back to Asha's house, drank some broth, and went to bed. Every night, my father called me before I went to sleep. We talked about everything except what caused the breach between us. He came to Yero's funeral but there was no sign of his ex-girlfriend, Evelyn, or his ex-boyfriend, Hugo. I was sure that Evelyn's mother told her what happened. I had to face the fact that Evelyn did not love me as much as I thought. She was obviously gone for good.

Daddy came to the hospital every evening and told Yero some tale involving good cops, crooked cops, stupid criminals, savvy criminals, and the underbelly of our great city. As always, Yero loved it. Daddy made Yero's last days a lot less painful and I'll always love him for that.

I'd lost twenty-five pounds because it was hard for me to eat

solid food. Sometimes I caught myself listening for Yero's footsteps. This was my new life. Pathetic, isn't it?

Life with Asha and Nick was interesting. He went away and
Asha was happy. He stayed away too long and she got antsy. When
he was actually here for days on end, Asha complained to me
about what a stick-in-the-mud he was and how much fun he was
before they got married.

She bugged him and bugged him until he bought her a new
car. It was not a fancy one but it looked good. He was furious that
she got into that accident and banged up his Mercedes, but Asha
just shrugged it off. "Your ass should just be glad that I didn't get
hurt," she told him.

Before Yero died, Asha had given me a check for ten thousand
dollars. I spent three thousand of that money catching up our
bills. Since I was in her house now and not paying rent, I tried to
give her back the rest, but she refused to take it. I reminded her
that Yero had life insurance on his job and a tidy little sum was on
its way to me. She still refused to take it back. Asha can be cruel
and selfish but she usually melts like wet sugar when I'm in trouble.

I was lying in bed reading the Bible when Daddy called to say
good night.

"Hey, sugar. You all tucked in?"

"Yes, Daddy. How are you?"

"I'm the happiest man in New York."

"Why?"

"Because my daughter is back in my life."

A lump formed in my throat.

"I'll never lie to you or mislead you again, Saundra. I swear it.
Do you believe me?"

"Yes," I whispered.

"Good."

"Daddy? Where are you really from?"

"I was born and raised in Dayton, Ohio. My dad was a janitor
and my mom was a housewife. I had three little brothers. Elwood,
David, and Buster. I don't know any of them anymore."

"Maybe we could find them."

"No, Saundra. Well, actually I wouldn't mind seeing my brothers. But it is hard for me to forgive my dad for throwing me out of the house."

"Did he throw you out because . . ." I couldn't finish the sentence.

"Yes. Because he found out I was gay."

Chapter 40

ED

I was surrounded by white. White carpet, white silk wallpaper with pictures, diplomas, and Keith with other celebrities staring at me from the wall, ensconced in silver Tiffany frames. The rest of my boss's furniture was glass, including his desk. He sat behind that desk now, listening intently as I brought him up to speed on the Nancy Rosa St. Bart investigation.

"Yesterday I spent a lot of time in Hercsville. I talked to a psychologist who treated Shareeka Ellison's kid."

"How old is he?" Keith asked.

"Sixteen."

"Think it might be him?"

"Could be," I admitted. "His girlfriend might have another female making the phone calls."

"They would have to be some real sick kids."

"Yeah. The dead animals would indicate serious mental problems."

"You mentioned a photo in the dog's mouth."

I crossed one leg over the other. "It was a picture of Nancy and Bruce standing in the front yard. Anybody could have snapped it."

"So what now?"

I sighed and told him the truth. "I've talked to the investigating officers. I talked to the guys who man the gate leading into Hercsville and I've come to the conclusion that the perpetrator lives in that town."

"Does St. Bart have any enemies?"

"None in town that she is aware of. She wrote a whole bunch of lists. Men and women from her past that might be holding a grudge. I took the list and checked every name out with the Hercsville phone company. So now I've run out of ideas. Do you have any creative suggestions?"

Keith frowned and tapped a sterling silver pen against the glass. "She needs to go live somewhere else until you figure this thing out. She shouldn't tell anyone where she is going."

"No chance of that. I asked and her answer was that she won't leave Denzel Washington."

He blinked in confusion. "What?"

I had to laugh as I told him about the wallpaper. He chuckled merrily a few times and then sobered up.

"This woman sounds like a nut. Maybe there haven't been any phone calls and she killed the animals herself or had someone else do it."

Chapter 41

SHAREEKA

Shareeka was thrilled about the party. She was tired of Day-shawn's new friends and their wives. Tired of eating entrees with portions that would hardly satisfy an eight-year-old, blocks of stinky foreign cheeses and handling thirteen-piece dinnerware for one fucking meal.

She remembered how they used to laugh in bed when Day-shawn came home to tell her about those knobby-kneed socialites with their Botoxed, superarched eyebrows telling him how much their sons loved his "gangster music." That's why it shocked her when he stopped laughing at those people and started desperately trying to become a tight-ass just like them. He ignored calls from his old crew and referred to any and every interest he had before he became a mainstream movie director as "ghetto shit" or "kids' stuff" with his nose all twisted up.

It was way past time to remind him of the fun they used to have back in the day so he could snap out of Gumbel-land by inviting all his old friends and a few famous people that were still street. Six months ago she had booked one hundred first-class tickets for their friends from Cali to be flown in, and they would be arriving at any minute.

Dayshawn would be home at about eleven this evening, and

when he got there he would meet a houseful of the people he had abandoned.

By the end of the evening, he would be ready to go home.

Dayshawn smiled wearily when he saw his driver standing in front of the airport terminal doors.

Fabian took the two carryalls from the aging skycap and put them in the trunk of Dayshawn's brand-new Rolls Royce 100 EX convertible as everyone stared. Most people stared at the car, others at the seven-foot-two bald-headed Nigerian driver. The fans pressed forward and Dayshawn signed autographs until he was sick of it.

He got in his car.

"How was your flight, Mr. Ellison?" Fabian asked in his thick Italian accent he acquired after immigrating to Rome with his family when he was six.

"It was all right, a little turbulence but okay."

"Oh, don't say that, don't say that. I'm like that guy, what's his name, from *A-team*? I hate flying, man. What was that guy's name? I used to love that show."

"Mr. T. How can you forget his name?" Dayshawn chuckled.

"I know Mr. T, I just forgot his character's name from the show."

"I think it was B.A."

"Yes! That's it! B.A.," Fabian said, snapping his large fingers and smiling into the rearview mirror.

"I'm so tired, I can't wait to take a dip in the pool, drink a little wine, and go to bed."

"I don't know about that," Fabian said, shaking his head.

"What do you mean?"

"Your wife made other plans. I cannot tell you anything more or she will be very angry and she don't like me already."

"What plans?"

"All I can say is that she was getting the house very pretty."

Dayshawn held up his hand. "All right, man. Say no more."

Dayshawn sighed, slid down in the plush seat, and turned on the television. He was tired, but he always appreciated it when Shareeka went out of her way to be sexy for him. If what Fabian said was true she got the kids out of the house, she was burning scented candles, and would probably be wearing some freak nasty lingerie when he walked through the door. He was a little jet-lagged from the flight, but he could definitely throw down. He closed his eyes and decided to take a short nap in preparation for the love-fest.

"Wake up, Mr. Ellison," Fabian said as he turned the corner leading up to his mansion.

"What the fuck are all these cars doing here?" Dayshawn asked angrily, leaning forward in his seat.

"Like I said, your wife made plans."

"Why didn't you tell me it was a fucking party?"

"You told me to say no more."

"Aw, man! I can't believe this shit."

Dayshawn could hear the music blaring and see people milling around outside his house. They were blasting The Gangbangers' first gold single, "Bros befo Hos."

He got out of the car and jogged up the driveway. A guy he didn't recognize stopped him for a pound.

"Yo, whassup!"

"Hey, how you doin?" Dayshawn said coldly, slapping his palm.

"Oh, you don't remember me?" the man asked, clutching a forty-ounce Guinness Stout.

"Huh?" Dayshawn asked as he watched three long-legged women in skimpy gold shorts munching mozzarella sticks as they walked by.

"I'm the kid from the old block they used to call Baby Hambone! I'm Rodney's cousin."

Dayshawn remembered Baby Hambone, but he wanted to forget the chain-snatching kid, his dust-selling cousin Rodney, and his sister Peaches, who didn't let her period or a yeast infection ever stop her from getting her groove on.

"Yeah, yeah, I remember. Have you seen Shareeka?"

Baby Hambone took a final swig from the bottle. "Yeah, she's in there."

"All right, man, I gotta go."

"Yo, I need to talk to you, man . . . I've been writing this movie—"

"That's cool, but I really need to get inside. Nice talking to you, man."

Dayshawn went inside and found the house filled with people. Weed and tobacco smoke filled the room as people from his old neighborhood danced to the music.

"Surprise!" Shareeka exclaimed when she saw her husband. She rushed forward and gave him a loud kiss.

Dayshawn blinked at the sight of all his old friends grinning and cheering amid the silver balloons.

"Oh, shit!" Dayshawn grinned. He moved forward, accepting hugs, handshakes, and back slaps.

"Yo, Bustacap!" a voice boomed from the crowd and a tall, skinny man with bad teeth pushed his way through.

Dayshawn grimaced at the sound of his old nickname. "Hey, Push," he said quietly.

"The guest of honor has just arrived, ya'll. Bustacap is in the muthafuckin' hizoussse!" the DJ shouted into the mic.

Shareeka watched her husband closely and couldn't figure out why his smile seemed so fake.

Push either didn't notice or didn't care about the lukewarm reception. He threw an arm around Dayshawn's shoulder and shouted, "I ain't seen this muthafucka in five years. He still my main man, though."

Everyone laughed and Shareeka grabbed her husband's hand as they were both enveloped by well-wishers. The music—old hits by The Gangbangers—was blasting from speakers that were strategically placed around the enormous ballroom. After she had greeted all her homegirls from back in the day, Shareeka slid away to check on the food. There were over a hundred people in her home. They were chugging Tanqueray and forty-ounce bottles of malt liquors, so stomachs would soon start to growl.

Three women in the kitchen were stirring two huge vats of collard greens.

Shareeka took in the collards, the pans of frying chicken, and the barrels of homemade potato salad. "Everything okay in here?"

The eldest, a woman in her fifties, wiped sweat from her forehead. "We workin' as fast as we can."

They were interrupted by Dayshawn, who stomped into the kitchen and glared at Shareeka. "Muthafuckas is runnin' all over the house, Shareeka. You need to git back on out there."

"Dayshawn, these ladies live over on Flash Place. They've been slaving away back here making the food."

Dayshawn smiled and shook their hands. "Thank y'all a whole lot."

Shareeka followed him back into the crowd.

"I can't believe you threw me a goddamn hood party," Dayshawn whispered between clenched teech.

"These are the people who stood with us when we had nothing, Dayshawn. You need to check yourself. Seriously."

Dayshawn sighed. "Well, all right. But I wish you woulda left Push alone. I don't like him up in my house."

Shareeka's eyes widened in surprise. "But Push was your boy. He was the first person I called."

Dayshawn shook his head. "Never mind."

Shareeka noticed that Push was watching them intently from across the room. "What's goin' on between you and Push?"

"Nothin'."

"Bullshit. Never mind, I'll ask him myself."

Dayshawn squeezed her arm hard. "Mind your own business. I'm not even playin' with you on this one. Stay the fuck out of it. By the way, how all these muthafuckas get here anyway?"

Shareeka pulled her arm out of Dayshawn's grasp. "I flew 'em out and sent cars to the airport to pick them up."

"You mean to tell me that I paid for all these round-trip tickets from Los Angeles to New York, and back, plus limousines?"

Dayshawn opened his mouth to say more, but their old friend, Layla, shouted, "Come on, you lovebirds, y'all got company."

Everyone laughed and then Dayshawn pulled his wife close. "Let's dance."

As they grooved to an old slow jam, Dayshawn whispered into her ear, "Shareeka, why didn't you hire a caterer?"

"Our friends don't want no catered food."

"You're wrong, baby. They're going to be disappointed. They

can eat this shit back home. They probably wanted to see a different way of life."

Shareeka wrenched her way out of his arms and fled.

More ghosts from his ghetto past appeared. In seconds he spotted Leah, who used to own the local pawnshop, MC Mezzanine, a wack rapper he used to smoke trees with back in the day, Shareeka's homegirl Patsy, and others.

Dayshawn wanted to run screaming from the house, but he had to put on a good front and keep pretending he was happy to see them all.

Shareeka stood in the center of the room wearing a tight red dress emblazoned with the Escada symbol on the front, what seemed like all the gold she owned hanging from her neck and ears, a crimped and curled hairdo with excessive baby hair swirling on her forehead, and thigh-high tan boots with the word GUCCI in block letters up the front with a rhinestone G hanging from the zipper.

Fifteen years ago she would have looked great to him, but now she looked like an idiot. He preferred his wife in feminine slingbacks and designer clothes that were not obviously made for lower-income people who had something to prove.

He waved Shareeka over. She made her way through the crowd and hugged him around his neck.

"I don't want to fight today," she whispered.

"Where are the kids?"

"Over at Nancy's house."

"We need to talk, come with me for a minute."

Dayshawn took her hand as everyone went back to smoking, drinking, and dancing. He tried not to notice all the roaches and cigarette butts he saw all over his nice things.

"You have to say hello to the people in the V.I.P. room first."

"V.I.P. room? What are you talking about?"

"I turned the theater into a V.I.P. room for the day. I knew those famous people didn't want to be around our peeps because they would start asking for record deals and shit, but they still wanted to come through."

Dayshawn felt his jaw tighten. "What famous people, Shareeka?" She winked. "You'll see."

As they walked upstairs past the flock of celebrity bodyguards they entered into a cleaner version of what was going on downstairs. A gigantic bowl of freshly rolled vanilla dutches was on display as soon as they entered the room. Shareeka passed one to Dayshawn, but he waved it away.

"I enjoy your party, why fuh nevah come to no rude boy event, cha know?"

It was the number-one reggae artist in the world, Tuddy. He was a Jamaican street kid with amazing skills who managed to hit the big time when a record executive discovered him while on vacation a few years ago. He wore a burnt orange silk shirt with silk royal purple pants, gators, and a raccoon hat. His grill was worth more than what the average American makes per year.

"Hey, Tuddy, good seeing you. I've just been busy."

Tuddy laughed. "Oh, so you a bizzzzeee boy, a bizeeee boy, right, right. Me no wanna hear no bumbaclot excuses seen. Next mont I wanna see yer ass in Jamaica. I man turn turty-tree."

"I'll do that."

Dayshawn saw three of the new and hottest gangsta rappers, Icon, Sauce, and Niteryder. They always gave him shout-outs on their albums that he didn't want. They were all drinking flutes of Cristal on the rocks, hood style, which meant that a few one-carat diamonds were thrown in the glass to make it taste better. Dayshawn couldn't believe he had funded this nonsense.

Shareeka was slightly drunk by now. She pulled Dayshawn into an empty bedroom and closed the door.

"Pull your pants down," she said, smiling wickedly as she began to hike up her dress.

"Are your crazy? What's the matter with you?"

Shareeka pulled down her dress and put her hands on her hips. "What's the matter with me? No, the question is, what the fuck is the matter with you? We used to do this all the time."

"Yes, when we were kids! When we lived in Compton. Why the hell are you dressed like that, Shareeka? Why are all these people here?"

"These people? What do you mean these people? You act like

you never seen them before. Did you forget that these are your people, Mr. Bustacap?"

"Bustacap? Aw, man, you just don't get it, do you? The people we left behind don't want to be there, Shareeka. They're there because they have to be there. The ghetto is not for black people. It is for poor people. And we ain't poor anymore."

"You really don't got no love for the hood no more, huh? All those premieres and black-tie dinners with crackers that wouldn't say shit to you a few years ago done got you fucked all the way up, haven't they?"

"I don't wanna hear that shit. My problem is you're still trying to live in the past. These are not our people anymore, Shareeka. Are you really enjoying this party or are you just afraid of change? Look at you, dressed like a sixteen-year-old chicken-head."

"Oh, really?"

"And look at your hair. I'm sick of this shit."

"This is how I looked when we fell in love."

Dayshawn began undoing the huge fountain of multicolored fake spiral curls. "Take that shit off!"

"Get off me!" Shareeka screamed as she tried to retighten the ponytail.

"And I want all these muthafuckas out of my goddamn house. Now!"

"What am I supposed to tell them, huh? That they gotta go 'cause they ain't Tom Cruise or some shit?"

"I don't care what you tell them."

Shareeka burst into tears. "I can't believe how you've changed."

"I can't believe how you haven't!" Dayshawn shouted.

He ran out the door and down the stairs.

"Busta! Come here!"

"Yo, Busta! Where's the bathroom?"

He pushed his way through the crowd, ignoring them all. Once outside, Dayshawn jumped into his car and sped off into the night.

PART THREE

THE CHERUBS

Chapter 42

ASHA

Sex had never been the end-all and be-all for me. I also liked poetry, candelight, and red roses. Subways and city buses had always been a no-no unless I was broke and riding solo. Even in my late teens, there was no way that a man could take me anywhere using public transportation. I learned early that the only way to avoid all the arguing about it and the accusation of being a "snotty, bourgie bitch" was to not date broke-ass men in the first place. I became accustomed to luxury and didn't really think about it much. That is, until Dayshawn Ellison came into my life. He took it to a whole new level. Shareeka had given me his cell phone number, but it took me a while to call him. It was one thing to tell people who didn't know any better that I was a production assistant, or a PA as they are known in show business. It was another thing to tell that lie to a movie producer/director with a string of films under his belt. He could probably sniff out the deceit before the conversation was halfway over. Thus, the hesitation. But it couldn't be put off forever.

"Hello."

"Dayshawn, this is your wife's friend Asha Seabrook."

"Who? How did you get this number?"

"You told her to give it to me."

"No, I didn't."

"Yes, you did."

"Look, miss. I don't have time to play games right now. What's going on?"

"Don't you remember? You, me, and Shareeka were out in back at your pool. She told you that I was an out-of-work production assistant and you said—"

He laughed. "Oh yeah. Sorry. Thought you was some groupie tryin' to get slick. So, whassup? How are you?"

"Fine."

"You're a beautiful woman. Anybody ever told you that?"

"Sugar, a whole lot of anybodys have told me that."

He laughed again. Heartily. "Yeah, yeah, yeah. I definitely remember you. A real confident, bodacious sister."

I didn't know what direction the conversation was taking, so I played it cool and professional. "Um . . . how can I get a resume to you?"

"Girl, you don't need to send me no resume. Shareeka say you do what you do. That's good enough for me."

"So . . ."

He thought a minute. "Let's get together and talk about it. Tell you what, I'll even cancel the plans that I already have for this evening. How is that?"

"Cool."

"Where are you?"

"Excuse me?"

"I'm in Midtown Manhattan right now. Where are you?"

"Oh. Home in Hercsville."

"Can you come into Manhattan and have dinner with me?"

Could Mike Tyson kick some ass?

"Sure."

"Good. You live in Hercsville, right?"

"Yes."

"Okay. Give me your address. I'll have a limo there to pick you up in about two hours."

"Please tell the car service to send one that has been freshly cleaned. I hate it when somebody else's funk is still in the back."

"Girl, what you talkin' about? This is one of my own personal limousines. With my own personal driver."

I didn't show any excitement.

"All right, but tell your own personal driver what I said. Okay?"

"White or black?"

"What?"

"Well, since you are one picky and discriminating lady, I'm asking if you would prefer a white limo or a black one."

"Black, of course. White is far too nouveau riche."

"Hmmm. I like that."

I rattled off the address, not wanting him to think that I had nothing else to do except make small talk on the phone with him.

"Thank you, Dayshawn. I have to run for right now."

"See you in a few."

"I wore a short, tight red skirt and a matching sleeveless blouse with the top two buttons undone so that Dayshawn could ogle my huge round breasts, which were straining against the thin cotton fabric. Even though I had no intention of cheating on Nick, there was no reason for Dayshawn to know that. I figured that I could keep him under control and fly up the film production ladder if he thought that there was even a slim possibility of getting me into bed someday.

It was a Friday evening. I left Saundra at home talking on the phone with her father. Nick was in Charleston. His plane was due in at midnight.

The limousine dropped me off at a French restaurant on Fiftieth Street. It was a classy but low-key type of place. It was also off the beaten path. Not a celebrity or media hangout.

He stood up as I approached the table and extended a hand in greeting.

His grip was firm. His eyes were glued to my chest. My eyes stayed on his face. He was a good-looking guy, not as stocky as he looked on camera. We both had a café-au-lait complexion.

He had broad shoulders, hair cut close to his head, and eyes that were so pretty they should have been on a girl. He smiled briefly and I caught a glimpse of pearly white teeth with a slight gap in the front.

Funny that I'd never noticed the gap before.

"Hello, neighbor."

"Hey, Dayshawn."

The waiter came and we ordered drinks.

"So how are Shareeka, Crenshaw, and Cheery?"

Dayshawn shook his head. "I'm not drunk enough to talk about it."

Uh-oh. Trouble in Ellison City.

"What do you want to talk about?"

"Why Asha Mitchell Seabrook won't go back to her career at Macy's Department Store. Why Asha Mitchell Seabrook wants me to give her a start as a PA in the movies."

I was cold busted. "Do you know what I want to talk about?"

"What? How you thought you could bullshit a businessman just because he used to be a Jeri Curl–wearing, fake gangster?"

He didn't look angry. In fact, his eyes were twinkling merrily.

"No, that is not what I want to talk about."

"What then?"

"What I want is the name of the private detective who did the background check for you. I think my husband might be cheating on me and I'm willing to pay a lot of money for the truth."

"Word?"

"Word."

He leaned back and ran his hand across his chin. "Damn. I'm sorry about that, girl."

"Thanks."

Muthafucka wasn't as smart as he thought. Nick wasn't cheating on me and I didn't need a private eye. What I needed was for this man to forget about my lies and start feeling protective of me.

"Listen, the guy that works for me is really expensive. Something like five hundred dollars an hour. But there is a private dick floating around Hercsville. He is looking into all this shit that has been happening to Nancy. His name is Ed Winsome. Shareeka can probably get you the number."

"Nancy is a real looney but she seems nice. What happened to her?"

"That wasn't nice."

"You don't think that wall-to-wall, floor-to-ceiling pictures of Denzel Washington in every single room of her house spells looney?"

He blinked twice. "What?"

"You've never been to her house?"

"No."

"Well, don't say that I'm not nice until you check that shit out. But enough about Nancy. I'm sorry that I lied to you. But everyone lies to get into show business, don't they?"

"True," he admitted.

I gave him my sweetest smile. "Please forgive me. It wasn't a real big lie. And it is the lowest job on a movie set. Barely pays minimum wage sometimes. Just think how much worse I could have behaved. I could have stolen a screenplay, had you produce it. The media would have a field day. Or I could have—"

He was laughing hard now. "Stop, stop. I get the point."

I stuck my lower lip out in a sexy pout. "I deserve to be punished." My chest heaved as I said this. My breasts were thrust forward. Way forward.

His voice was husky now. "Yeah, girl? What kind of punishment?"

I whispered, "I'll work on the set for free. No salary at all."

He sipped his drink thoughtfully. "What about overtime?"

"No problem."

Dayshawn Ellison smiled a nice-to-know-that-I-can-fuck-you-any-time-I-want-to smile.

He had no idea who he was dealing with.

The waiter returned, breaking the sexual undercurrent of our conversation.

He ordered steak *au poive* and a bottle of Cristal champagne for us to share. I chose grilled salmon and Caesar salad.

We made small talk until the food arrived. I named all the books that I'd been reading about working in the movie business. Told him that I didn't want to be a department store accessories buyer anymore because offices were too confining. Claustrophobic. He told me how much he'd fallen in love with the energy of New York and how he dreaded returning to California. Parts of his next movie were being shot there. The other locations were Cleveland, Denver, and Rome.

"Sounds interesting. What is the movie about?"

"This upper-class black couple embezzle some money from his company and go on the run when the FBI comes after them."

"Doesn't sound like the Dayshawn Ellison productions that I've seen. You've been doing urban comedies. This sounds dark. Why the switch?"

"I have to prove that I can do something besides, come on in, buy some popcorn, and let the hood rats make you laugh. Do you want to know something?"

"What?"

"Those Hollywood guys gave me hell. They don't like to finance a black movie unless it is a comedy. That is, unless it's some black men shooting at each other ghetto gangsta flick. Shit pisses me off."

"From what I've read, Hollywood is about the dollar. And only about the dollar. Do those comedies and gangsta flicks make more money than regular dramas?"

"*Waiting to Exhale* made money. That was a drama."

"Then why did they give you so much trouble?"

"They say that *Waiting to Exhale* was a fluke. That it can't happen again."

"So this film has to make money."

"Correct."

His mood was starting to shift from up to a most definite down. I switched gears.

"So, what happened to Nancy that she needs a private eye?"

He ran down the phone calls. The dog. The rat.

I lost my appetite and put my fork down. "That is the craziest story I've ever heard."

"For real. Anyway, now Penelope won't let Thelma come to my house anymore and I can't say I blame her. Shareeka has also stopped Crenshaw's therapy sessions over something Penelope said about him. Can't blame her either. She got him somebody new, a guy this time. He works a few towns away . . . can't remember the name. It doesn't matter. Crenshaw seems to like him."

"What is Crenshaw's problem? If you don't mind my asking."

He sighed. "Too rich. Too spoiled. Who knows?"

"Isn't that something? If you're poor, that's a problem. Too much money is a problem. You can't win."

Dayshawn observed me for a moment. "You're a good listener."

"Thanks."

Here it comes, I thought. Sooner or later, every married man starts bitching about his current wife or ex-wife.

"I can't talk to Shareeka. Do you want to know what she did?"

"No."

He told me about the hood party. He was so angry and the scenes he described sounded so ridiculous that I couldn't help laughing. Not just laughing. I really lost it. Hood rats running through his mansion waving forty ounce bottles of beer and shouting Bustacap! Shareeka removed her waist length blonde weave for the occasion and replaced it with a glazed hairdo that she had worn at sixteen! Tears flowed from my eyes. My arms were wrapped around my stomach, my body moved back and forth on the leather seats.

"Please don't get mad, Dayshawn," I gasped. "I'm sorry."

He chuckled. "It was some real unbelievable shit. But you know what? I've decided not to worry about it. Me and you are going to stay on the road as much as possible and leave your husband's cheating ass and my wife's crazy ass here in New York."

He winked at me.

I smiled back.

"Asha."

"What?"

"I wanted to jump your bones the minute I laid eyes on you."

"What's stopping you, baby?"

Yee hah! Bustacap . . . one of the finest, most talented men on the fucking planet, wanted to knock boots with me.

He laughed. "You're a trip, girl."

"So I've been told. Do you have to go home tonight, Mr. Ellison?"

"Nah, I do what I want. What about you?"

I beckoned to him to lean over the table so that I could whisper in his ear. "My panties are getting wet."

Homeboy got the check paid and me out of that restaurant in record time.

Over the next six hours, we worked our way through two bottles of Cristal, told each other some personal stuff, and fucked in every position imaginable.

By the time the limousine pulled up at my door, I was his new production assistant. The movie which was called *The Last Sunset* started shooting in a month.

Chapter 43

SAUNDRA

Unable to get out of bed.

Unable to do more than shower once a day, brush my teeth, and get back in bed.

Unable to eat anything heavier than soup.

Unable to stop thinking about Yero lying under six feet of dirt and how cold he must be.

Unable to rest, knowing that Yero's spirit would never find peace until my physical body died and I sped through the universe to hold his hand.

Unable to care when Asha brought me the news that my job was gone. I had been fired for failure to report, failure to call in, failure to answer the telegrams, and worse, telling my boss on the phone that fashion no longer meant anything to me at all.

Unable to stop calling Daddy several times a day just to talk about old times when Yero was alive and Evelyn was my substitute mother.

Unable to give a damn about my personal safety when Asha's doorbell rang one evening and a man I had never heard of asked to speak with me.

I was home alone. I opened the door.

"Hello, my name is Ed Winsome. I'm a private investigator. Are you Asha Seabrook?"

"No."

"Do you know where I can find her?"

"She went to dinner in the city."

"May I ask who you are?"

"Saundra Brown. Her sister."

"May I come in, Saundra?"

"Are you looking for me?"

"Well, no. I was hoping to speak with Asha."

"She's not here."

I was about to close the door.

"Asha could be in a lot of danger. May I come in?"

Asha in danger? My heart started to race and I led him into the newly decorated living room.

He looked around. Checking out the silk-covered walls, pale green carpet, African art on the built-in bookshelves. Huge blown-up photos of Asha at every stage of development hanging on the walls. The sofa, which was also pale green. The heavy tables and floor-to-ceiling lamps.

"May I sit down?"

"I don't really care."

He sat down. I sat down.

"What kind of danger are you talking about? Or did you just say that to get in and kill me? If that's the case, just do your strangling or shooting."

He eyed me quizzically. "Is everyone crazy in this town?"

"What?"

"I'm a licensed private detective. I'm trying to prevent a murder, not commit one."

I touched my locks nervously. "I'm not crazy. Just very, very tired. Who might get murdered and what does it have to do with Asha?"

"Has she received any threatening phone calls or unusual mail that frightened her?"

"Not that I'm aware of. Who would do something like that and why?"

"That's what I've been hired to find out."

"Mr. Winsome . . . I can't do a cat and mouse. I really can't. Who hired you and how does my sister fit into it?"

"Well, Shareeka says that there will be a six-page story about the case in tomorrow's *Hercsville Democrat,* so I can tell you now without violating any privacy codes."

By the time he finished telling me about Nancy St. Bart's home, the fake love relationship she had with her mother, her burglar brother with the fluffy cheeks and cherubic face, plus the dog, the rat, and his lack of leads, I had forgotten all about my problems.

"Jesus! Why would this person want to hurt my sister?"

"Don't you see? Shareeka is Nancy's friend. Asha is Nancy's friend. I'm worried that your sister might be next on this woman's list."

It took me a few minutes to process it all.

He watched me intently.

"This is awful. That poor woman. She must be scared out of her mind."

"Unlike you."

"Huh?"

"You're a woman who invites would-be killers into your home."

"Do you want some coffee or tea?"

"Before or after the strangulation?" He was teasing me and his dimples showed.

"Well, you better take it now," I replied dryly. "Once I'm strangled, you'll have to make it yourself."

"I'd like tea. May I follow you into the kitchen?"

"What for?"

"So that you can take my mind off this case for five minutes by telling me why you're so down in the dumps."

"My husband just died of leukemia. I'm homeless. I'm jobless. I'm living with my sister once again. It is the second time I've landed on her doorstep in two years."

He whistled. "I'm really sorry."

Most people say that as a matter of course, but Ed Winsome really meant it. He suddenly looked very sad.

I stood up. "Come on. Let's make the tea and figure out who is terrorizing poor Nancy."

We decided to stay in the kitchen. Over bites of whole wheat muffin and sips of peppermint tea, he told me that the woman he'd hoped to marry had just dumped him because he had taken too long to propose and she'd found someone else. If he couldn't solve the case he was working on, it was going to look very bad for Keith Williams, who prided himself on winning every time. Worse, he didn't believe that Nancy was doing this to herself and feared that he had overlooked an important clue.

"She needs a pop-in," I said.

"A what?"

"You need to know beyond the shadow of a doubt that this woman is not up to some tricks of her own. So far, you have called each time before going to her house. I think we should pop in on her and see if you learn something."

"We?"

I told him that for some reason, I suddenly needed to get out of the house. A drive in a car with fresh air coming in the open windows might make me sleep better later on.

"This doesn't sound like a good idea. She is wary of strangers. I don't want to upset her unnecessarily."

"Then I won't get out of the car. You go in alone."

"And leave you outside when someone is running around in the middle of the night planting dead dogs?"

"It's still light outside," I reminded him. "If I see anyone, I'll honk the horn."

"I still don't like it."

"Poor little dog. Poor little rat. Whoever did this needs to go to jail for the rest of their lives just for harming defenseless creatures."

"That's very sweet," he said quietly.

I could feel the tears welling up. "It's just so cruel."

His voice became gentle and soothing. "Hey, hey, Mrs. Brown. Take it easy."

I felt embarrassed. "I'm sorry. It seems like I do nothing but cry lately."

"And for good reason. Well, I can't leave you at home in this condition. So you can ride with me if you want to."

"Thanks."

"By the way, who did your sister go to dinner with?"

"Dayshawn Ellison."

"Why?"

"He is making a movie and she wants a job on the set."

"Hmmm . . . interesting. Have you ever met him?"

"Not yet."

"Not a fan?"

"I used to be a big fan. It just doesn't seem important anymore. Nothing does."

"How about possibly saving your sister from a deranged psycho?"

"Let's go."

Chapter 44

PENELOPE

Thelma sat staring morosely at her plate while her mother cut a thick slice of roast beef for her.

"How was school today?"

"Fine," Thelma said absently.

"Have you looked at those college catalogs that came in the mail last week?"

"Not yet."

"Have you told Crenshaw Ellison that you won't be visiting his home anymore but that he is welcome to come over here?"

"Don't you have some meeting to go to, Mama? Or some other kid's head to shrink? I hate being questioned like this."

Penelope almost cut her own finger off instead of the roast beef. "Thelma! What has gotten into you?"

"Yes, I have told Crenshaw."

"You'd better watch the way you talk to me, young lady."

"Or?"

What? She must have heard wrong. "What do you mean, Thelma?"

"You said that I'd better watch the way I talk to you. I asked you what the penalty would be if I don't."

When Thelma said this, she was sitting up straight and staring her right in the eye. What the hell was wrong with Thelma? In spite of her training as a mental health professional, Penelope was also an angry parent and so she said the first thing that came to her mind.

"The penalty will be that you won't be living here any longer, smart-ass. You'll be in upstate New York at a private girls' school, repeating the eleventh grade because they don't take seniors. You'll be as far away from Crenshaw Ellison as my limited funds can take you. Now, how do you like that?"

Penelope turned away with a hurt expression on her face and placed roast beef and mashed potatoes on both their plates.

Thelma kept her eyes on her plate. "I know that you've been hoping that we'd break up. I'm sorry, but that is not going to happen."

"Oh, really?"

"Really."

Penelope nearly choked on a forkful of mashed potatoes. "Well, we'll just have to see about that."

"Mommy, I—"

Penelope pushed her chair back, stood up, and threw her napkin down on the table. "What? You what, Thelma? I'll tell you what! Your grades are slipping. Your priorities are definitely not straight. And do you know why, Thelma? Because all you think about is that silly boy. He has money, Thelma. He is going to be okay no matter what. But you? You need to graduate at the top of your class and get into a top-tier school. I know you're not paying attention to me right now. But I'm going to put a stop to this madness once and for all."

Thelma picked the napkin up from her lap and wiped her lips delicately. "I hope this fancy boarding school takes babies, Mommy, because I'm not having an abortion."

Penelope held on to the back of her chair with both hands. "Babies? What the fuck are you saying, Thelma?"

She had never uttered such an obscenity at Thelma before. She saw the shock on her daughter's face and did not care.

"I'm pregnant."

Chapter 45

THELMA

Miss Thelma Brewster knew perfectly well that she was not pregnant. She watched her mother recoil in horror, burst into tears, and run up the stairs without uttering a sound to comfort the woman who had nothing but her best interests at heart.

Adolescents are a selfish bunch.

She went into the bathroom and used her cell phone to call Crenshaw. She told him what she had just done.

"So are you pregnant or not?"

"Haven't you heard a word I said?"

"Yeah."

"Then you know that I'm not pregnant."

"Why did you do that?"

"So that she'll let me start coming back to your house."

"How do you figure that?"

"Don't you see? First, she stops me from coming to your house. Six weeks from now, she'll stop you from coming here. Then you won't be able to call me anymore. Then she'll take my cell phone away if you do call. I saw how it was all going to go down and I put a stop to it. Now, what difference does it make whether I come see you or not? The damage is already done."

Crenshaw started yelling. "She didn't stop you from coming over here because she doesn't like me. She stopped you from coming over here because a maniac sent my mother a cut-up rat. If I had a kid, I'd do the same shit. What you did is really wild. I didn't know that you could lie and scheme like that."

"You just don't get it, do you?"

"Get what?"

"What happened over there is just her excuse. She has wanted us to break up for a long time."

"I don't believe that. We met every single week for a year and she never said anything like that."

"Your damn daddy was paying her close to four hundred dollars a session!"

She was sorry as soon as the words left her mouth. Now he was hurt.

"I gotta go, Thelma."

"I'm coming over."

"No. Don't."

Chapter 46

NANCY

Eric Collins had found her a new gig. Well, she'd have to do a screen test, but he said that the producers were really hot on her and not to worry about it. It was a feature film. She was to play the part of a single mother, worried about her son who was being courted by a gang at school. The script had passed her scrutiny in that there was no mammyish or ghetto dialogue. The mother was educated, employed, and well spoken. The pay was above union scale and the movie was going to be shot in California. That meant she could get out of New York and away from the maniac that was stalking her.

Jaleesa had just served her dinner in bed. Macaroni and cheese, ribs, collard greens, and apple cobbler.

The television in her room was turned to a cable channel that was showing a rerun of a Spike Lee joint called *Get on the Bus*. Shareeka ate, watched the film, and thought about what a carefully crafted film it was and wondered why black folks had not come out to support it the way they should have.

She was an hour into the film when Jaleesa appeared in the doorway. The young woman seemed upset.

"There is a man and a woman downstairs. Ed Winsome and Saundra Brown. I told them that you had retired for the evening, but Mr. Winsome says he needs to see you."

Nancy smiled. "Sure. What is the problem?"

The girl hung her head and muttered, "I didn't say there was a problem."

She went back downstairs.

Nancy pulled on her jeans and a T-shirt. Who was Saundra Brown?

Ed and the strange woman were waiting for her at the bottom of the stairs. The woman was very tall, dark skinned, and pretty. She wasn't wearing any makeup, her locks were very long, and she was wearing a beige cotton shift dress with plain Birkenstock sandals. Most interesting in Nancy's eyes was that Saundra Brown was not looking at the Denzel photos. Most people stared at them and then started asking stupid questions.

Nancy greeted Ed with a kiss. "I didn't know you were coming."

Ed replied, "Sorry for the pop-in but I was nosing around town, asking questions, and decided to check on you. This is Saundra Brown. I believe you've met her sister, Asha Seabrook?"

Asha's sister.

Nancy shook the woman's hand. "Yes, your sister is a fun person. We've spent a lot of time together, mostly at Shareeka's house."

"It's a pleasure to meet you," Saundra replied with sincerity. "I just moved in with Asha recently. I'm sorry about your troubles."

Ed cleared his throat. "Nancy, who is the young woman who answered the door?"

"That's Jaleesa. I told you about her. She cooks and cleans for me."

"Is she a family member?"

Nancy looked startled. "Of course not. She lives over on Flash Place. Shareeka recommended her."

There was silence.

"What's the matter?"

Ed asked gently, "Nancy, have you ever noticed that Jaleesa looks exactly like Randall?"

"My brother Randall?"

"Your brother Randall."

"That's ridiculous," she sputtered. "Whatever gave you that idea?"

"Jaleesa opened the door and I almost fainted. For a moment, I thought it was Randall dressed in drag. I asked Jaleesa if she was your cousin and she just ran up the stairs. For some reason, she got very upset."

Nancy didn't know what to do. What to think.

"Let's go into the living room. Would you like some refreshments?"

Ed looked pensive. "No. We're not staying. What I do need is Jaleesa's full name and address."

Chapter 47

SHAREEKA

Her weave was back in place. Her house was once again neat and orderly. Her marriage was a wreck. Dayshawn stayed out of the house as much as possible. They spoke only when absolutely necessary. Shareeka missed Thelma's afternoon visits. She also worried about Nancy. The security, because of what had happened, was still tight.

Shareeka was not in the mood for a hysterical phone call from Penelope, but that is what she got.

"Did you know about my daughter's condition?"

"Thelma doesn't visit anymore. Remember?"

"Crenshaw could have told you."

"Told me what?"

"That . . ." Penelope began to cry. Loudly.

"Is Thelma sick?"

"Is she sick? She'd be better off right now if she had diabetes."

"Penelope, could you please put Thelma on the phone? I'm worried about her now."

"I will not put Thelma on the phone. She is in this condition now because of you and your family."

Thelma must have received something terrible in the mail.

"Oh my God!"

"Damn right."

"What did that maniac send to Thelma?"

"He sent her a baby! A baby! Her life is destroyed. It's over!"

Shareeka suddenly felt nauseous and faint. "A dead baby?"

"It isn't dead, you idiot."

"The woman who has been stalking Nancy sent a living baby to Thelma in the mail?"

"What are you talking about?"

"Penelope, don't throw out any more insults. I am not an idiot. Stop crying, tell me what you're talking about, or get the fuck off my phone."

"Put Crenshaw on the phone."

"I will not."

Penelope suddenly stopped sobbing. "Wait! Thelma admires you even though I don't know why, and Crenshaw is your son. Maybe you can talk some sense into them. Surely you can see that two sixteen-year-olds are not ready to raise a child."

Shareeka put the phone down and yelled, "Crenshaw! Get your ass down here right now!"

Cheery came running in. "Crenshaw fell asleep."

"Go wake his ass up and tell him to get down here. Now."

Cheery took one look at her mother's angry face and fled.

Shareeka picked up the receiver. "I didn't know anything about this. You are saying that Thelma is pregnant, right?"

"Yes." It was a whisper.

Crenshaw entered the room. "What?"

"What? Thelma's mother is on this goddamned phone. She says that Thelma is pregnant. Why I gotta hear it from her, Crenshaw? Why didn't you tell me?"

A weird expression appeared on Crenshaw's face. He appeared to be struggling with some major decision. Finally, his shoulders slumped. "I didn't know until tonight."

Shareeka went back to Penelope. "I need to talk to my son. I'll call you back."

"Please encourage them to do the right thing. I'll pay for an abortion. It won't cost you a thing. Surely you can see that Thelma and Crenshaw shouldn't be in charge of a baby? Please."

For once Shareeka and Penelope were in full agreement.

Chapter 48

ED

Flash Place was a black ghetto located on the far side of Hercsville. I made sure that my gun was fully loaded and readily accessible before I climbed out of my car. I had done my homework. There were no apartment buildings. Just lots of tiny houses, built close together. These dumps were mostly rentals. The lady who owned most of them was Janice Webster, publisher of the *Hercsville Democrat.*

The rich, black folks on the other side of town had to know that most of these streets were unpaved, that the garbage cans on the corner were overflowing, and that most of the residents' minimum-wage paychecks went to pay Janice Webster's ridiculous rent.

Was there a difference between getting screwed by a black landlord instead of a white one? Should there be a difference?

Janice Webster was a slumlord. I felt disgusted.

Jaleesa Crisp lived in the dumpiest of the dumps. The steps on the gray weather-beaten house sagged beneath my weight. I knocked on the door and Jaleesa answered.

"I'm Ed Winsome. Do you remember me?"

"Yeah. What do you want?"

"I just want to talk to you. Can I come in?"

"No. My mama is asleep."

"Okay. Then why don't you step outside and talk to me a little bit? As you know, I'm trying to help Nancy St. Bart. Someone has been threatening her. I'm sure you want to help your employer. Right?"

Jaleesa and I went down the steps together. I was hoping that they wouldn't collapse, sending us both into the bowels of the earth.

She was wearing black cutoff shorts, a black tank top, and sneakers, no socks. She crossed her arms and waited without speaking.

"Have I done something to offend you, Jaleesa?"

"No."

"Then why are you looking so mad?" This wasn't some detective-type trick question. I honestly wanted to know what her problem was.

She shrugged. "I'm going through some stuff. Nothing to do with you."

"I can understand that."

"What you wanna ask me?"

"Do you like Nancy?"

The answer was no. I could see it on her face.

"Sure. She treats me good."

"Who do you think is behind those threats?"

"Somebody who don't like her."

Miss Jaleesa was a cagey little thing.

"Does your mother know Nancy?"

The answer was quick and sharp. "No. They never met."

I followed my instinct and told a big lie. "Oh. Nancy is really sorry about that. She plans to pay your mother a visit to make up her lack of manners. After all, you work very hard. The least Nancy can do is stop by to say thank you."

Jaleesa Crisp took off running. Back into the house. The door slammed. I heard the click of the lock.

There was absolutely no reason that I could see for the panic in Jaleesa's eyes or for her dash back into the house.

I walked calmly back up the steps and banged on the door. "Jaleesa. Open up."

Nothing.

Another knock. "I'm not going away. I hope you call the police on me. Go ahead and do that, Jaleesa. I think they'll want to talk to you about what has been happening to Nancy."

The door was opened by a woman in a wheelchair. She was thin, middle aged, dark. When her mouth opened, I saw a lot of teeth. Her legs were covered with a raggedy plaid blanket.

"I'm Francine Crisp. Stop all that bangin' on my damn door. Jaleesa don't feel good. She went to lay down."

"Bullshit."

"What did you say?"

"I said bullshit. Tell Jaleesa to get out here right now."

There was no fear in Francine's eyes. "No."

"If she doesn't get out here in half a minute, this place will be swarming with more cops and detectives than you can imagine."

"Go 'head. I ain't done nothin'."

I stared her down. "Jaleesa has. Or she knows something about the crimes."

"What crimes?"

The mother was not lying. She clearly didn't know what I was talking about.

"Mrs. Crisp, do you know Nancy Rosa St. Bart?"

"We've met. Yes."

"When?"

"None of your business."

"Do you know that someone recently threatened her life?"

A glimmer of something appeared in her eyes. "No."

"Well, I think Jaleesa knows something about the dead animals."

The woman frowned and smoothed the plaid blanket. "Dead animals?"

I was quickly tiring of the Crisp family. "What is wrong with your legs?"

"I was in a car accident a few months ago. I'll be up and around soon."

As soon as you get the insurance company check, I thought.

"Good-bye, Mrs. Crisp. I'll be back soon."

She watched me go down the stairs.

On the last step, I turned around. "Your daughter got upset last night because I asked her if she was kin to Nancy. She said no. It's all very strange. Jaleesa and Nancy's brother Randall look like twins."

The door slammed shut.

Chapter 49

SHAREEKA

Dayshawn had hit the roof! Of course Thelma had to have an abortion. Anything else was just plain crazy. He lit into Crenshaw with an anger that left the boy reeling. Shareeka intervened before he actually punched the boy out.

He left the house the next morning with both his children in tow. A silent, angry Crenshaw and a scared Cheery. He would drop each of them at school and then keep on going into Manhattan to do his work.

That left Shareeka at the kitchen table reading the papers. Dayshawn's name was on Page Six, the daily gossip column that appeared in the *New York Post*.

Apparently, Dayshawn "Bustacap" Ellison's love of beauty (remember his triple-platinum "My Bitches Is Fine" way back in the day?) hasn't gone away. It just might lead him straight into a divorce court if he isn't careful. The ex-gangsta rapper turned movie mogul was seen last night canoodling with the wife of a soul food heir. According to our sources, at one point her breasts were practically in his plate during their intimate dinner at a Manhattan bistro last night. His spokesman told us that the woman in question is just a neighbor and potential employee. Yeah. Uh-huh. Sure. We believe you, Busta.

Shareeka closed the paper and rubbed her eyes. Over the years, she had read hundreds of these blind items. At first, she used to get upset. Throw things at Dayshawn. Accuse him of cheating on her with his woman in town. He got tired of hearing it. She got tired of yelling.

For a brief moment, she considered calling Asha but then decided against it. The press didn't care who they hurt as long as they sold papers. There was nothing to the story at all.

It was the price she and Dayshawn had paid for all the money, the house, the music, the fame.

Chapter 50

ED

"Jaleesa didn't come to work today, did she?"

"No," Nancy replied. "How did you know that?"

"Because I went out to her house yesterday. When I started asking her questions, she got scared and ran in the house. She knows something, Nancy. She might be the key to unraveling this case."

"Why would Jaleesa want to scare me?"

"I don't know. I called you right away but you weren't home. I wanted to pick you up and take you to the Crisp house."

"Why?"

"Because Jaleesa told me that you and her mother have never met, but the mother says that you did. I want you to look at the mother."

"What is her name?"

"Francine Crisp."

"I don't know anybody by that name."

"Maybe you know her by another name."

"Possible."

"So I'm on my way to pick you up and we're going over there. Okay?"

"Okay. Where are you now?"

"About five minutes from your house."

"I'll be waiting outside."

She got in the car without saying much. I drove fast, saying even less. We reached Flash Place in fifteen minutes. Nancy gasped as she looked out the window at the hopelessness, the poverty, the desolation. "This is just plain terrible. It looks like the worst part of Red Hook in Brooklyn."

I was surprised at her surprise. "You've never been over here before?"

She shook her head.

I made a left turn and then a right. We were in front of the Crisp house.

I held my client's elbow as we walked gingerly up the steps and then knocked hard on the door. It swung open. We went in.

There was nobody there. Someone had cleaned up and cleared out in a hurry.

Chapter 51

NANCY

That night, Nancy lay in bed talking to her brother. She told him all about the Crisps.

"Randall, do you have a daughter?"

"Nancy, you know I ain't got no kids."

"Think hard, Randall. Maybe you don't know you got a kid. Jaleesa is about nineteen years old, which would make you about that same age when she was born. Who were you dating back then?"

"I was still with Tracey, but she never had no kid. Even if she did get pregnant and didn't tell me, she didn't have no kid. She must have aborted it if she ever was pregnant."

"How do you know that?" Nancy insisted.

"Because she still lives with her mama in the same place. She never left the old neighborhood. Do you think that this girl looks like me?"

"I didn't until Ed Winsome said it. Now it's all I can think about."

"Don't you think that you would have noticed that before he did?"

"I never really looked her full in the face, I guess."

Randall chuckled. "Ah, the rich. I used to do some laboring work for people like that. They said good morning. They said good night. They said Merry Christmas. But they never really looked at me."

"Thanks for the sociology lesson, Randall."

"What do you want me to do, Nancy?"

"I didn't have no baby, Randall. I have never been pregnant. Ever. So you must have been sleeping with somebody."

"Why did it have to be me? That bastard could have kids all over the world."

That bastard. Their father.

Maybe Jaleesa was his child with a woman named Francine Quick. Maybe Jaleesa hated her because she had to live on Flash Place while Nancy lived in relative splendor.

But that had not been Jaleesa's voice on the phone. Maybe it was Francine's voice. Maybe Francine knew all those things about her family because that bastard had talked about them. The woman had simply been lying when she told Ed that she and Nancy had met.

It all made sense.

Nancy didn't feel like talking anymore. She hung up on Randall. Then she went upstairs and washed her hands exactly one hundred times.

All of a sudden, she hated Denzel. It had been his job to keep the demons out of her house. Now the demons were back. The childhood flashbacks would start again soon. He had failed. There was only one thing left to do.

Tomorrow she would buy a gun.

Chapter 52

ASHA

The *Hercsville Democrat* gave full rein to Nancy's story. If that wasn't enough, Saundra filled us in on her evening ride with Ed Winsome.

Nick was horrified.

We were lying in bed, wrapped in each other's arms. It was good to have him home. I missed him.

"Baby, I'm not leaving you and Saundra to go back out on the road until this fool is caught."

I kissed him on the neck and shoulder. "Hmmm . . . what did I do to deserve such a thoughtful husband?"

Now that he had his old job back, Nick was once again the man I'd married. Except for the sex. He wasn't adventurous anymore. Even now, he kissed me on the head and kept on talking.

"For real, Asha. This is crazy. I can't believe we left the city for this."

Okay. No sex this morning.

"Tell your mother to buy us a house somewhere else."

"Ha-ha. Very funny."

"Well, I just won't open any mail. You can do that. I'm not answering the phone. You can do that, too."

"Did you see the sparkle in your sister's eye?"

"What are you talking about?"

"Please don't tell me you didn't see her talking all fast and stuff when she mentioned Ed."

I took a moment to consider it. Yes, she was a lot more animated than I'd seen in a long time. "Don't say anything to her about it, Nick. Don't tease. Don't signify. Ignore it. Maybe she doesn't notice that she enjoyed talking to him. Maybe it wasn't even anything about him. This guy has a puzzle to solve and it is exciting in a sick kind of way. If you say something, she'll probably feel guilty about not thinking enough about Yero and go right back to where she was. Promise me."

"You're right. My lips are sealed. What can we do to get him back over here?"

"Nothing. If he likes her, he'll show up on his own. If he doesn't, he won't. Leave it to the universe."

"Now you sound just like her," Nick teased.

I kissed him on the lips.

This time he responded.

Chapter 53

ED

I sat in my office the next morning with the phone pressed to my ear listening closely as Nancy rattled off her theory.

She sounded happy that the mystery had been solved, so I did not tell her that the team of paralegals employed by Keith Williams had worked their wizardry and decided that the name Crisp was a phony. Worse, I had gone back to the house without Nancy. The wheelchair had been left in a back bedroom. Which meant that the older woman could walk. Why did she want everyone to think that she was sick or handicapped?

Nancy was in more danger than ever because whoever was behind all this had to know that time was running out.

I planned to go back to Flash Place again. Maybe someone there had snapped a picture of the older woman. At a block party. A baby shower. Somewhere. My instincts told me that the woman had not lied when she said that Nancy knew her. There was a strong possibility that Nancy would recognize the photo and that she did know the lady . . . just under a different name.

When Nancy hung up, I thought about Saundra.

Actually I had thought about Saundra quite a lot since our first meeting. She was a beautiful person. A compassionate earth mother who had lived a holistic lifestyle until the death of her husband. She had cracked me up in the car with tales of her

clashes with Asha over the organic food, meditation, yoga and belief in universal law.

Yero had been a smart man. This lady was a keeper and I wanted
to get to know her better. Common sense told me that it would be
a long time before she was ready for a romantic relationship but
maybe my puzzle could help lift her depression. After these kooks
were off the street, maybe I could just ask for her friendship. Maybe
she would accept my offer.

But first, I needed a conversation with Dr. Penelope Brewster.

I dialed her number and she answered on the first ring. Her
voice was as crisp and efficient as I remembered.

"Dr. Brewster, this is Ed Winsome. I'm the private detective that
you met at Shareeka Ellison's house."

"Yes. How are you?"

"Not too well, Doc. I need to pick your brain for a minute."

"Okay."

I told her everything from beginning to end.

"Doc, I feel that the answer to this puzzle lies somewhere in
that Denzel wallpaper that covers her house. Why do you think
Nancy decorated her house in that way?"

"To keep something out."

"What?"

"Whatever goes on in her head, Mr. Winsome. I'll bet Nancy
used to have visions before she put up those pictures."

"Visions of hell or the anti-Christ or something?"

"No. Flashbacks of some terrible trauma that occurred in her
life. The Denzel pictures have absolutely nothing to do with the
celebrity himself. It is a coping mechanism. I can't explain it in
detail now. It is a very complex psychological problem. Just know
that she doesn't have the flashbacks, daydreams or night dreams
right now. If the pictures of Denzel come down, they start all over
again. It is a private hell. My heart aches for her."

"Is it possible that she is sending these packages to herself and
not receiving strange phone calls at all?"

"No. She clearly is a troubled woman who needs help but I got
the impression that Nancy really does not know who is behind
all this."

"What about the tormentor. Why doesn't she just step to Nancy and have it out? Or, step up the requests for money?"

"This isn't about money, Detective Winsome."

"I figured as much."

"This is about the desire to harm Nancy physically in the most gruesome way possible. She is in a great deal of danger and I hope that you catch this individual and prevent a terrible tragedy."

"Thank you, Dr. Brewster. You've been a big help."

"Glad to be of service."

It was a relief to hear a mental health professional say that Nancy wasn't causing all this ruckus for some crazy reason that we didn't understand. I suddenly wanted to hear Saundra's voice.

Her voice sounded sleepy but I plunged ahead. The case was weighing me down and I needed her to hear me. I told her about Francine and Jaleesa Crisp. I told her about Nancy's theory but not about my conversation with Dr. Brewster.

"Nancy's theory is too pat," she replied. "Too easy."

"I agree. So what do you think I should do next?"

"Why ask me? You're the expert."

"Well, the pop-in was your idea and it bore fruit."

She chuckled.

"So, I thought you might have another good idea."

"Actually, I'm thinking about Nancy and all those pictures on the wall."

"What about them?"

"Did you ever see *The Omen*?"

It was an old flick. About a young boy who was really the devil sent to earth. The first one was a hit so, naturally, Hollywood brought out a couple of sequels.

"Which one?"

"The first one."

"Yes. I remember it."

"Remember the guy who papered his wall with religious pictures to keep the bad energy outside?"

"Yes."

"I think that the Denzel images mean the same thing to Nancy."

"Not possible." I lied.

"Why not?"

"Because, according to everyone that has been inside that house, those pictures were there long before Nancy received the first phone call."

"No. No. No. You don't understand," Saundra said.

"Enlighten me." I wanted to hear what she had to say and whether it would match what Dr. Brewster had said.

"The images on her wall have nothing at all to do with what has been going on."

"So how does that help me?"

"Maybe it won't," she admitted. "But all I'm saying is that Nancy was not at peace. This is not a case of a serene soap-opera star suddenly victimized by an unknown tormentor. Nancy had a tormentor long before she got that first call, and the images soothe her in some way. She feels they protect her in some way."

"How do you know all this? Psychology major in college?"

She sucked her teeth. "Western thinking? No. I studied all kinds of Eastern philosophies, fables, and religions. I did it on my own. Well, not exactly on my own. My father's girlfriend was into all that. She taught me a lot."

"So maybe this tormentor from long ago is the one behind the phone calls. Is that what you're saying?"

She sighed. "Linear, Western thinking. It is so, so limited."

I playfully made my voice humble and peasantlike. "Please tell me, oh Great One. Tell this caveman what the moon is trying to reveal."

She laughed. "Boy, do you sound silly! I really don't know what is going on, but something was troubling Nancy enough to put those pictures all over the place like that. In fact, she probably prays to them."

This wasn't funny. "Prays to Denzel Washington for guidance?"

"Not just that. He is like Jesus to her. He gives her protection and guidance."

"Then she is definitely crazy."

"That's not the point. If dead animals are being left on her steps, she must feel that Denzel has let her down."

"Denzel as a Jesus-like protector. I've heard it all now."

"Well, you have to admit that he is cuter than the picture we have of Jesus."

"Saundra," I teased. "That is blasphemous. Aren't you afraid of going to hell?"

There was a beat.

"No, Ed. And, I'll tell you something else . . ."

"What?"

"Nancy has lived in hell for a long, long time."

Chapter 54

THELMA

Her little stunt had backfired and she didn't feel so smart any-more. Crenshaw was curt and angry every time she got him on the phone. He wouldn't let her come over, which really pissed her off because not being able to go to his house was what led her to such desperate measures in the first place. Penelope walked around the house like a zombie most of the time. She had can-celed all of her appointments for the next two weeks. When she wasn't marching through the house with vacant eyes, she was lec-turing Thelma on the perils of teen pregnancy or going over to the newspaper where she sat with Janice for hours at a time.

Thelma knew that Penelope had not told her grandmother about the pregnancy. There was nothing in that for her but a tri-umphant sound from Janice's throat. Thelma could imagine the scene. Her mother crying. Looking for solace. Janice raising her hands toward the sky. Vindicated. "I told you that the apple don't fall far from the tree," she would say. "Father a thief. Daughter a tramp."

Thelma wished that they both would get run over by a truck. But in the meantime, she had to think of a way to get back in Crenshaw's good graces. School would be over in two days and she didn't want to spend the months of July and August sitting home alone.

She sat hunched over her math homework. The numbers danced before her eyes. She couldn't take it anymore. She picked up her cell phone and it rang.

"Thelma, it's me."

"Hi, Crenshaw."

Thelma was happy. It was the first time in days that he had done the calling.

"Hey, sweetheart."

"Girl, you gotta talk to my mother and your mother. You gotta tell the truth and make this thing right. I can't take the pressure anymore."

"But, but . . ."

"What do you plan to do, Thelma? Sit there and pretend to be pregnant for the rest of your life? Don't you think somebody is going to wonder why your belly stays the same size?"

Thelma hadn't thought of any of it. She hadn't planned to lie and say she was pregnant in the first place. Spite, immaturity, and a stubborn determination to have her own way had caused this whole mess. If her mother had not barred her from Crenshaw's house and then mentioned sending her away, it would never have happened.

"Let's go away somewhere. Come on, Crenshaw. Let's just get in your ride and head for some place where we can be left the hell alone."

"Listen at you," he said in disgust. "Talking about running away like we're two little kids or something. I don't know what to think about you anymore, Thelma."

She was suddenly scared. "What does that mean? Don't you still love me?"

"I'm not sure. You scare me now. How do I know that you haven't told me a pack of lies while we been together?"

"But that's crazy. I love you."

"Do you love your mother?"

She did. Deep down inside. She did. "Yes."

"But you told her a pack of lies, right?"

She was trapped. "I'm scared to tell her the truth. She might kill me or something."

"Cut the drama. Dr. Penny is not going to kill anybody."

"Stop calling her that. She isn't your doctor anymore."

"Fine. Just tell her."

"You tell her."

"What?"

"You heard me."

"Thelma, I'm not telling your mother anything."

"I meant tell Shareeka. She'll call my mother and spread the news."

"Hell no! You started this mess, Thelma. Now fix it. I'm not talking to you anymore until you do that. Understood?"

"Understood," she whispered miserably.

Chapter 55

PENELOPE

Because of the tornado that had swept through her home, ruining the image she had of her daughter, Penelope no longer cared whether Hercsville expanded or not. She had called everyone involved to say that they didn't have to come to any more meetings. The committee was no more. In fact, the more Penelope thought about it, she wasn't sure she even wanted to live in Hercsville anymore. There was no way she could stay here throughout Thelma's pregnancy and have everyone snickering behind her back.

Helping her mother down at the newspaper office had given her something to do. Something to take her mind off the awful fact that Thelma was not a virgin. Not only that she was not a virgin, but she was pregnant with that hood rat's child. All of her beautiful dreams for her only child had vanished.

Worse, the two child-parents refused to even consider an abortion. She and Shareeka had been calling each other almost daily. Crenshaw wasn't saying anything. No matter how much Dayshawn and Shareeka ranted and raved, he kept his head down and said nothing. Penelope had put on her psychologist's hat three days ago and advised them to stop. Give Crenshaw a chance to think about everything they had said.

Now she entered her home, dropped the keys on a table, and headed upstairs.

"Mama."

The small voice came from behind her.

Thelma stood there wearing a pitiful expression. She had been crying.

"What is it, Thelma?"

"I need to talk to you, Mama. Please sit down."

Penelope prayed that Thelma had decided to have the abortion. She sat.

Thelma paced.

"Mama, I have something to tell you and you're not going to like it."

Penelope put her head in her hands. "Go on, child," she said wearily.

"I'm not pregnant."

"Thank you, Jesus! Was the first home pregnancy test defective? You did another one today and the results were negative?"

"I never even thought I was pregnant, Mama. I made it all up because you stopped me from going over to Crenshaw's house."

"What? The two of you cooked up this scheme and upset everyone just because of that?"

"It gets worse."

"How can it get any worse? Shareeka and Dayshawn are worried sick. I'm surprised at both of you."

"Crenshaw didn't have nothing to do with this. When I told him what I'd done, he got real mad at me. Now he doesn't trust me anymore. He's not even sure he loves me anymore. He said so himself."

Penelope scrunched up her nose like she smelled something bad. "You have got to be kidding me."

"I'm not. I'm sorry, Mama."

"You know what, Thelma?"

"What?"

"I was wrong about Crenshaw. He is a smart boy, after all. He is smart not to trust you anymore. I know that I don't."

Thelma plopped down on the sofa and started howling.

Penelope knew that her daughter wasn't crying about the fractured mother/daughter relationship. She was crying because she had lost her man.

Penelope left Thelma there on the sofa and went upstairs.

Chapter 56

NANCY

The gun was lightweight, fully loaded, and fit neatly into her purse.

She sat in the garden area of Manhattan's chicest restaurant listening to her agent's gossip about the industry and its players.

"Nancy, are you listening to me?"

"Yes, Eric." She gave him a dazzling smile. "Don't I always?"

"Most of the time," he chuckled. "I admit that Fab Floor Shine wasn't one of my better ideas. I'm glad you turned it down."

She made a mental note to be even nicer to Eric in the future. He was a decent man and a good agent. She had told him the story of Francine and Jaleesa Crisp. They both agreed that the mystery had been solved and she could stop cutting checks to the firm of Keith Williams and Associates.

"Now, I want you to go to the audition tomorrow. Your appointment is at noon."

"What audition?"

Eric hit the table. "Nancy, you begged me for months to get you in to read for the new Denzel Washington movie. The audition is tomorrow. At noon. Here is the address." He pushed a piece of paper in her direction. "Do not be late."

Denzel.

She had no more faith in him. If her demons weren't so powerful, she would tear all of his pictures down. But he kept most of them at bay. There had been a time when the house never seemed to have enough light, no matter how many lamps she bought. She had been unable to stand the sound of a news broadcast for fear that a child molestation case would come up. She still didn't watch the news, but at least her heart didn't beat as fast if someone else was watching it and she didn't have to leave the room. She had been unable to listen on the phone if one of her girlfriends was talking about her "first time."

Denzel had helped her in a lot of ways. She shouldn't be mad at him because he had let the Crisps get through. Yes, she would be on time for the audition and give him a note (he wouldn't want his staff to know all his business, so she couldn't blurt it out loud) that explained how the gun would protect her from Francine and her crazy-ass daughter. She would explain that he was free to concentrate on making his next movie a smashing success.

Chapter 57

ED

Saundra's theories kept me up at night, so I tried them out on Randall the next morning. He could help me. I sensed that. He remained tight-lipped. So I tried another tack.

"Will you ride with me out to the place where the Crisp women lived?"

"Thought you said they was gone."

"They are gone from that house. Perhaps they moved to another. You look so much like Jaleesa. I just want you to ask around a little bit. See if you can get either a new address or a picture of the mother from someone."

"Yeah. I'll do that. When?"

"Now."

"How am I supposed to get out to Long Island?"

The cherub was really pissing me off. Did I have to spoon-feed this idiot?

"Get on the Long Island Railroad. Get off at the Hercsville Station. I'll pick you up in my car and drive you there. When all is said and done, I'll drive you home."

"Cool. See you in a few."

"Thanks."

"Yo, Ed?"

"What?"

"Did my sister tell you that she bought a gun?" He laughed. "She got something for they asses."

"Randall, your sister is not mentally stable enough to own a gun. Why didn't you call me right away?"

He sounded sad. "Guess I thought it was a good thing."

"When is the last time you talked to her?"

"This morning. She called me and Mama. All excited because she is auditioning for Denzel Washington today. As a matter of fact, now that I think about it, she said you wasn't working for her no more."

"Then that should tell you something. I'm no longer getting paid but I'm hard at work anyway. Why? Because I feel that your sister is in more danger now than she ever was before."

"Damn." He sounded scared. "We gotta do something."

I had a flashback.

"Prays to Denzel Washington for guidance."

"Not just that. He is like Jesus to her. He gives her protection and guidance."

"Then she is definitely crazy."

"That's not the point. If dead animals are being left on her steps, she must feel that Denzel has let her down."

My God!

"Where is that gun, Randall?"

"I guess it's with her. Why would she buy a gun and leave it home?"

"Did she say where that audition is being held?"

"No. What's wrong?"

"Get on the train, Randall. But get off at Penn Station here in Manhattan, not Hercsville. I can't explain now. Just do what I tell you."

Chapter 58

NANCY

After all these years, she and Denzel Washington were going to be in the same room together. In the flesh.

It was exciting beyond belief.

Nancy showered fifteen times. Washed her hands thirty-five times. Then she dressed carefully. Her hair was combed a little differently. More of a loose wavy style instead of the pageboy.

She was reading for the part of Ophelia. A judge who was faced with a moral dilemma and had to struggle with her conscience all the way through a high-profile criminal trial. That meant looking smart, official, judicious. A black suit, sheer stockings, pumps, and pearl earrings would have the desired effect.

Part of her wished the Crisp ladies would show up right now. Then she could put some bullets in their conniving, jealous asses and not have to worry about them as she read for the part in Denzel's movie.

She looked out the window.

There was no sign of Jaleesa.

The house was getting messy. It was time to get a new cleaning woman.

Nancy admired her hairstyle in the mirror, tucked the gun into her purse, and then sat down to write him a note.

Dear Denzel:

It is a pleasure to meet with you today. To actually be in your physical presence. Thank you so very, very much for protecting me all these years. I don't blame you about the Crisp women. I know that you have been very, very busy trying to put this movie together. So you fucked up. Don't worry. I forgive you. Everyone fucks up sometime. But I have a gun. Yes, as I stand here, watching you read this note, I have a gun in my purse. Take care and I'll talk to you again in my upstairs bathroom.

Love always,
Nancy

Chapter 59

ED

Ipicked Randall up outside Penn Station. The audition was being held on the sixth floor of an office building on Seventh Avenue near Fifty-third Street. Nancy's agent told me that. He sounded worried about my call, but there had been no time to explain what was going on.

Seventh Avenue goes downtown, which meant I had a choice. Get entangled in a midday traffic jam on Eighth Avenue or do the same thing on Avenue of the Americas. I chose the latter to avoid the Port Authority Bus Terminal and Times Square.

Randall's face was tight, closed, and worried.

Mine probably looked the same.

"Why did you change the plan, man?"

"Because we're going to the place where your sister is reading. To make sure that she doesn't do something stupid."

"Ain't it more important for me to find out where these two women are?"

"Listen, Randall. I have a friend who has a theory. She believes that Nancy put all those pictures of Denzel on her wall to protect her from whatever demons dance in her head."

He moaned.

This guy knew all about those demons.

"But then, it might have gotten out of hand. She might have

come to believe that Denzel could protect her from being harmed by other people."

"Well, he ain't doin' a good job, is he?"

"Exactly."

I looked Randall dead in the face and then turned back to face the traffic.

"Shit!"

"You got it, buster. He let her down. She might take a shot at him."

Randall's cherubic face collapsed and he started to cry. "Isn't there a faster way to get there?"

"The subway would be faster if we knew for a fact that the trains are running smoothly. Last week, there was a sick passenger on another train. It kept my train stuck in the tunnel for an hour. Can't take the chance."

He pulled at my arm. "Ed, it is twenty minutes to twelve. We're not going to make it."

He was right. I parked the car right where we sat, which was in a bus stop, didn't worry about the trouble I would be in for that, and ran like hell.

Chapter 60

NANCY

She waited in a small room with six other actresses whom she recognized from various soaps and TV commercials. Someone had made quite a spread for them: salad, sandwiches, fruit, juice.

They were all too nervous to eat or speak to each other.

Everyone just sort of smiled and studied the script one last time.

A perky red-haired assistant was calling each woman in, one at a time. Nancy wondered what the setup was.

She didn't have to wait long to find out.

"Nancy Rosa St. Bart!"

"Good luck," a fortyish sister in a pink suit said with a smile.

That was really nice. Seeing as how they were both up for the same job. Some people were so nice.

Nancy smiled at the woman. "Same to you. Have a great day!"

The door closed behind her. She followed the perky girl through a door.

"Just stand behind the white line and read when you get the signal," the perky girl instructed.

There he was.

It was a classroom setup.

The audition space was where a teacher's desk would normally be. A white line was painted on the hardwood floor so actors would know where to stand.

For some reason, two cops were standing in the back of the room. Behind all the chairs. Nancy assumed correctly that it was due to the fact that a major celebrity was in an ordinary office building and any nut could wander in.

There were many people sitting in different rows. Chatting. Making notes. Probably the screenwriters, financiers, and some other business types.

He was sitting in the first row.

She stood behind the white line and recited the lines so brilliantly that everyone in the room started clapping.

Nancy was thrilled. She pulled the note out of her purse. It was only four or five steps to Him.

He took it with a smile.

She stood there while he read it.

He stood up and yelled.

Something had gone terribly wrong.

The two cops and everyone else in the room rushed toward her. She tried to explain that everything was okay. That the Crisp sisters had not really done her any harm. But no one would listen.

Someone grabbed her purse.

"Yup. There is a gun in here!"

Ouch!

Her face hurt when she was slammed to the floor. In fact, her fat stomach felt like it was going to pop.

Ouch!

Her fat arms were roughly pulled around her back and handcuffs snapped on her wrists.

Dragged to her feet.

Half walking. Half carried out the door, into the elevator, and out into the street where a police car was waiting.

"Nancy!"

She twisted her head to the side and saw Randall huffing and puffing toward her. Then she was pushed inside the car and the door was slammed shut.

What the hell was Randall doing in Manhattan at her audition? she wondered.

Chapter 61

ED

They were holding her at the Rikers Island prison without bail. Even though she had not removed the gun from her purse or threatened him in any way.

I understood but it still felt bad just the same.

Things got better when Keith got involved. But not by much. He tried to call in some favors, but even though his judge friends agreed that Nancy needed a good psychiatrist more than a prison cell, none of them wanted to be the person who set her free to take aim at an American hero.

They ran for cover.

He was working like a demon.

Every time I passed his office, I heard him arguing on the phone.

"Where does it say in the note that she wants to hurt him, intends to hurt him, or has asked someone else to hurt him?"

Or.

"Fine. I'll take that. Off Rikers Island and into a mental hospital for ninety days' observation. What do you mean that you don't want to sign the orders? Have some balls, man."

I had to smile. This was the type of fight that Keith lived for.

He won and Nancy was transferred to Bellevue Hospital's mental ward two days later.

When it became clear that no criminal charges would be filed against Nancy and she wasn't going to jail, I relaxed a little. Meanwhile, the stand-up comics were making merry about the note.

Jay Leno asked: Will someone please tell what Crisp women are? Do they snap in half like Lay's potato chips?

The audience roared.

A shock jock started ending his show with: "Forgive me if today's show was boring. Everyone fucks up sometime."

It went on and on.

Meanwhile, I kept working. Someone had called Nancy and threatened to kill her. Someone had killed those animals. Someone was still a danger to Nancy whenever she got well and was walking the streets again.

I sent Randall to Flash Place to see what he could find.

Chapter 62

SHAREEKA

Nick, Asha, Dayshawn, and Saundra spent one Saturday watching the whole media circus at the Ellison house. They watched all the network coverage, then switched to CNN, which was doing round-the-clock reporting on what was being called DenzelGate even though the actor had done absolutely nothing wrong.

A few talking heads on Larry King wondered aloud if there had indeed been a friendship between the soap opera actress and the leading man. Not necessarily something romantic or sexual. Just a friendship. After all, they were entertainers and it was not far-fetched to think that their paths had crossed at one time or another.

Denzel behaved like a gentleman. Said he didn't wish to press charges. That he hoped she would get some help. That she was a good actress and he wished her well. Then he stopped talking about the incident and started issuing a terse "no comment" whenever someone shoved a microphone in his face.

Shareeka was amused that Nick kept looking at Dayshawn out of the corner of his eye. He was starstruck and it was embarrassing his wife. Asha kept elbowing him in the ribs. Nick would stop. For fifteen minutes.

She also couldn't stop watching the two sisters and wondering why the two were so different. Asha was clearly engaged by the media extravaganza.

Saundra was just sympathetic to Nancy's plight.

"I got the impression from Ed that this was a pro bono case for Keith and that she doesn't have much money," Saundra announced.

Shareeka hadn't thought about that. She looked over at Dayshawn and he smiled at what she was thinking.

"Nancy is our friend," Shareeka said. "Dayshawn, can you contact Keith Williams and tell him to get Nancy into a private hospital? Some place nice. With great psychiatrists, beautiful rooms. Tell him to make sure there are a lot of trees and grass around. Nancy likes that."

Saundra actually got up and gave Shareeka a hug.

"The universe will bless you for that," she said.

Shareeka hoped that Saundra would stay in Hercsville for a long, long time. She could use a friend to replace Nancy.

It was clear to her now that Dayshawn wasn't going back home.

She looked at him. He was sipping his beer and having a good time.

His glance fell on Asha and Shareeka saw the heat and passion in her husband's eyes. The type of lust that can drive a man crazy enough to leave his wife and family. The type of flame that seeps into a man's soul. No outsider can extinguish that. It has to burn itself out.

Chapter 63

ED

Randall stayed in a fleabag motel on the worst side of Flash Place and worked the streets for a week before he hit pay dirt.

As I suspected, the two women had simply moved from one dump to another.

He snapped a picture of them as they were shopping in a grocery store.

"The trouble is," I told Saundra and her family "no one can get in to see Nancy until her psychological evaluation is over."

We were having Sunday brunch at her place. I didn't care for Asha. She was a little too self-centered for my taste. But Nick seemed to be a great guy.

All of them were hanging on to my every word. Folks like to have behind-the-scenes information.

"Not even her lawyer?" Nick asked.

I shook my head. No.

"How about Dayshawn?"

"Asha, why would they let an entertainer in the hospital if they won't let Keith Williams see her?" Saundra asked impatiently.

We all put some more buffalo wings and salad onto our plates. Asha poured more champagne into everyone's orange juice except Saundra's. She didn't drink alcohol.

I was digging her more and more. She let her hand touch mine just for a minute and I knew that she was into me too. We were celebrating the fact that Saundra had been rehired at the last place she'd worked. Asha went to see the boss and explained just how hard Saundra had been hit by Yero's death.

"To rap for the patients," Asha explained. "Seems to me they could use some cheering up."

Nick laughed. "So Dayshawn just raps his way over to Nancy, puts a picture under her nose and runs away if she starts freaking out."

It had been a stupid but really humorous suggestion.

They started squabbling in a good-natured way. I chuckled whenever one of them said something particularly funny. This felt good. They felt like the warm, close-knit family I had left behind to come East.

I didn't want to leave.

But I had to.

Something just occurred to me.

"Randall knows who the woman in the picture is," I said aloud.

Startled faces turned in my direction.

"How do you know that?" Nick asked.

"Why didn't he say something?" asked Saundra.

I stood up. "Don't know. But it is time to go ask him."

We said our good-byes but everyone knew that I'd be back to check on Saundra.

His mother wasn't home and I didn't ask where she was. When Randall opened the door, I didn't even ask to come in.

"Who is the woman in the picture?" I asked.

He shifted from one foot to the other. "She used to be a friend of Nancy's. When we were in junior high school. Her name is really Minnie Stewart."

"Why did you lie to me?"

"I didn't lie. I just gave you the picture and didn't say anything."

"By saying nothing, you knew that I would assume you didn't recognize her. That is called a lie of omission."

He didn't answer.

"Does Minnie Stewart have a reason to hate your sister?"

"Yeah."

"Tell me what it is."

"Ask her. You know where to find her now."

"Why can't you tell me."

He started to back up. "I don't tell Nancy's secrets."

Poor Randall. He had clearly been saying that for most of his life.

"Even if it will save her life?"

"Look, man, Nancy ain't never getting out of that hospital. She is out of danger." His eyes grew misty. "She has peace now."

"Just tell me what Nancy did to Minnie Stewart and you'll never see me again."

He sighed. Looked at the ceiling. Decided to give me the bare minimum.

"Nancy knew that one of the men who used to hang around our school was a pedophile. She saw that he was making friends with Minnie. But she didn't say anything. She didn't try to save Minnie at all, even though they were best friends. Minnie disappeared from school. She ran away from home. The rumor was that she was pregnant. As far as I know, Minnie and Nancy never saw each other again."

Jaleesa and Randall looked exactly alike. It wasn't hard for me to figure out who the pedophile was in all of their lives.

My eyes met Randall and we both knew what I knew about his and Nancy's father.

"Why did Minnie call your mother a coward? Was it because she did nothing to stop what was happening to Nancy?"

Randall shook his head vigorously. "No. Mama didn't know anything until it was way too late. Minnie must have heard Nancy call Mama that. Nancy used to say that a lot."

"Why?"

"Because Mama was too afraid to ask for details. Our lives were just supposed to go on like the mental destruction never happened. Nancy never understood that if Mama knew the down and dirty details, it would kill her. Mama is just protecting herself. She is nobody's coward."

"Do you know the down and dirty details, Randall?"

"No. It would kill me, too."

All of a sudden, I didn't want Minnie to go to jail. She had been there long enough. What I planned to do was get hold of her and Jaleesa and scare them good. Keith would help me with getting them into the interrogation room of a local precinct along with a couple of friendly cops. They needed to understand that if they didn't get off the East Coast and forget about ever contacting Nancy again, I'd find a means of putting them away for good.

But for right now, they could enjoy their small piece of justice.

A CONVERSATION WITH ANITA DIGGS

Q. Shareeka Ellison is an unhappy woman, despite her wealth. Who or what was your inspiration for this character?

A. The wives of the rap stars are like these hidden women in our society. We don't even know their names. I just wondered what the life of someone like Dr. Dre or Ice Cube's wife would be like and then made it all up.

Q. Didn't we meet Keith Williams in one of your previous novels?

A. Yes, he was the attorney who represented Jacqueline Blue in *A Meeting in the Ladies' Room*. I really like writing about him, perhaps because I was such a Johnnie Cochran fan. Someday, I'm going to do a Keith Williams novel and really get to know him.

Q. Why didn't you show us more interaction between Saundra and Phil?

A. I know that readers wanted to see them go back to their old, cozy ways but that just rang false to me. It will take many years (if ever) before they are close again.

Q. Will Nancy really spend the rest of her life in a mental hospital?

A. Only if she chooses to. Nancy can be helped and go on to resume her life and career. But, she may not want to do that. Real life is hard for her.

Q. Will Nancy's mother go and visit her?

A. Of course. Kate loves her daughter and vice versa. Kate, Randall, and Nancy are all victims of a very, very sick man. I hope that readers feel as much sympathy for Randall and Kate as they do for Nancy.

DENZEL'S LIPS

ANITA DIGGS

ABOUT THIS GUIDE

The questions and discussion topics that follow
are intended to enhance your
group's reading of this book.
We hope they provide new insights and
ways of looking at this wonderful novel.

DISCUSSION QUESTIONS

1. Why do you think that Nick married Asha?

2. Discuss what Asha and Saundra have in common.

3. Is Ed Winsome the right man for Saundra? Why or why not?

4. Will Asha take Dayshawn away from his wife?

5. Why doesn't Shareeka confront Asha and her husband as soon as she realizes that something is going on between them?

6. What did you think of Shareeka's party?

7. How do you think Jaleesa has been impacted by her mother's trauma?

8. Is Penelope a good mother?

9. Why couldn't Penelope really see who her daughter really was?

10. Will Crenshaw take Thelma back? Should he?

Dear Reader,

Greetings from Harlem! I hope you've enjoyed *Denzel's Lips* and will take the time to read *The Other Side of the Game, A Mighty Love,* and *A Meeting in the Ladies' Room.* All of these books have heroines who are uniquely unforgettable.

I've started lecturing high school students about careers in writing and publishing. It is really gratifying to see how hungry our children are for information. To learn more about The High School Project, go to my Web site, *www.anitadoreendiggs.com*

Thanks for your continued support!

Anita